To Joanne,

Be wii
big. becc
realit

_come

Of Magic & Lies

Book One: The Gatemaker Series

Maggie Brown

Maggie Brown

For anyone willing to dream...

Contents

Note from the Author.

Hello it's Maggie here, to warn you that this book deals with themes that could make some readers uncomfortable. If you do not like Spicy or violent scenes in your books then you should turn away now, otherwise you have been warned.

This book is the first book in The Gatemaker Series and will be part of a larger universe of books. However each series can be read alone or together.

I have chosen to write this book in British English so please remember that this may make some spellings look wrong or unusual. If you do feel that you have found a mistake in this book then please, please, please do not report it but message me with your concern.

Thank you for delving into my world of The Gatemaker. I hope that you enjoy my book.

Happy Reading.

Chapter One

Alyssa

Strange creatures fill the room, some look almost human if you can ignore the pointed ear-tips, animistic features or their otherworldly beauty. Others have leaves instead of hair, or bark-like skin and one has what looks like water swirling around her body as she twirls in a man's arms. Then there's the enchanting music that floats around the hall, it plays under the laughter and conversation that bubbles through the room. Everyone's happy, enjoying the party. Except me, as I stare across the room over all their dancing heads from my small throne on the dais.

Stifling another yawn and rolling my eyes at having to attend yet another damn event. Anger flashes through me when a dancing couple passes by, or another young suitor asks me to dance again. I'm rolling my eyes yet again when I see him. Mister tall, dark and handsome. I know he's dangerous from the glint in his eyes and the shadows swirling around his lithe frame, but I can't pull my eyes away from him.

I'm entranced.

He stops across from me! Standing on the edge glaring across the swirling mass of dancing couples, his dark fringe sweeps down, covering one of his twinkling blue eyes. The other remains locked on my face as I stare at him. Unable to move I watch as he pushes it back, revealing his handsome face and my heart stops beating for a second, as we gaze at each other.

I know who he is and I should stay away from him!

Everyone says he's evil, just like his father. But I'm walking before I even know it, pushing through the dancers to get to him. I don't react to any of the shocked gasps or startled shouts, all I want is him.

He's mine! My mind shouts at me, urging me to yell it at the party-goers as they get in my way. Suddenly there he is looking down at me as the whole room goes deathly silent. I'm lost in his gaze as his shadows play around us. Everyone else thinks he's dangerous but I know the truth.

Smiling, I reach up to brush my fingers across his cheek as he leans towards me, "Princess." He mocks with his melodic voice, staring into my eyes as goosebumps erupt over my skin. My eyes fall closed when his lips brush my earlobe and he whispers, "found you!"

I muffle my sob behind shaking hands, as I bolt upright in bed, with tears rolling down my cheeks. Leather and Lavender fills my nostrils when I take a deep breath. *It was just a dream,* I tell myself silently as I try to draw in a deep enough breath, to ease the tight band around my chest. "It's not real." I mutter aloud to my empty room. Forcing myself to believe the words as the crushing pain of losing someone very important rips through me.

It's stifling this imagined agony of having had my heart broken. *What the hell do I know about heartbreak?* I'm the bloody weirdo that's never dated anyone or even been in love! Yet my mystery dream man—who doesn't even exist—makes me feel this way every time I sleep. How can I feel this intensely for a figment of my own overactive imagination?

Looking at the now familiar faded blue walls of my dorm I absently rub my chest, still feeling the connection to the man in my dreams. Every time I wake from one of my dreams I have the niggling feeling that they're somehow real, as though I've lived each one.

Yeah, crazy I know! There's no such thing as demons, fairies or any supernatural creature for that matter. No Otherworld that holds secret balls and trains their princesses how to fight and dance. And certainly no Magic. My life's as boring as a nuns. It isn't real! I tell myself again remembering what Rebecca my old therapist used to tell me.

"That world isn't real, Alyssa. He isn't real," she'd say twenty times a session, "it's all a construct you've created to try and explain the gaps in your past." So why does it feel as if I could reach out and touch that world I've created in my dreams, live in it even.

Shaking my head at myself for being so stupid, I grab my phone from the night stand and glare at the time. Urggg, I have two hours until my shift at Society. Groaning again I throw back my covers, shivering in the chill as the October air hits my sweaty skin.

I quickly run through my favorite yoga poses, stretching out my tight muscles before sliding my feet into my rainbow bootie slippers and almost running as quietly as I can to the shared bathroom down the hall. I don't want to bump into my dorm mates.

I mean they're nice and all, but I'm not one of them and I haven't got the patience to decline yet another invitation to join them in the bars and clubs of York. The loud catcalls and general hubbub of partying students on their way out to the student union float up to our second floor dorm, making me shiver, as I once again wonder what was wrong with me?

All my life I've felt detached from normal kids my own age. Their carefree attitude to just live in the moment, without a care in the world has always mystified me. I've never been able to fully let down my guard around anyone, even my adopted family. Always looking over my shoulder, waiting for the other shoe to drop or living in my fantasy world, always scared of anyone finding out just how broken my mind is.

Three years ago I was found unconscious in the woods by Jason Jones—now my best friend, ok my only friend—wearing some outlandish dress and when I came around a day later in the hospital I had no memory of who I was, where I was from or most importantly what had happened to me. I had no marks on my body, I hadn't been violated in any way, it was as though I'd simply appeared from nowhere.

No one had reported me missing, so with the police stumped and local authorities running around like headless chickens, Mrs Jones had agreed to take me in.

"Just until they find your family Dear," she'd explained calmly to me as I rocked in my thin gown, clawing at my thick auburn hair. But no one ever came forward to claim me. So they're the closest thing I have to a family even if they are considered a little odd by everyone else's standards.

Dream man's face flashes before my closed lids as I splash cold water on my warm face, making me groan as I once again remind myself; *he doesn't exist.* This is why I haven't had a boyfriend. I tell myself, that none of the boys at school, college or even at this university can measure up to the man in my dreams.

Looking into the mirror above the sink, I stare at my stormy blue eyes I silently repeat my mantra; *he's just a dream!*

"Always got yer head stuck in a book, little nymph," Lilah's voice says fondly in my head. She'd utter the same thing every time I missed dinner or was late getting up.

Letting out a shaky laugh I study myself in the mirror. I look like shit. My ivory skin is paler than usual, and even the bags under my eyes had bloody bags, thanks to the limited sleep I've been getting. Between my dreams, job and uni I can say I've officially kissed any decent sleeping pattern goodbye.

"You're beautiful, Alyssa." I hear Mrs Jones' musical voice ring clearly through my head, as if she was standing next to me. Just like any mum she always seemed to know when I was self-conscious.

"Then why doesn't anyone like me?" I'd ask back. To which she'd tell me I had a unique beauty that no-one else understood, but one day someone would.

Staring at my face in the mirror I smile as I remember her explaining to the then sixteen-year old me that it didn't matter what others thought, as long as I was happy.

Shaking off the bitter sweet memory and my latest dream I jump in the shower and half an hour later I'm standing back in my room, my hair tamed into two corn-weaves, wearing my black society shirt, short black skirt and calf high boots almost ready for my shift. Quickly applying some black eyeliner and mascara I appraise myself in the mirror. Happy with how I look, I shudder at the thought of yet another shift, working sucked.

Who thought bar tending would be such a good job? Oh yeah me, that's who. I scoff at myself, grabbing my jacket and keys. Society would be heaving tonight with it being Halloween I think with a shudder, *at least the tips will be decent*, I remind myself. Slamming the dorm door closed, I bounce down the stairs and out into the night.

I've taken two steps down the small dark path heading towards the city center when a loud wolf-whistle from behind almost gives me a heart attack. Confused, I hesitate, my muscles locking up as fear and adrenaline race through my body at the sound. *What a pig*, I think to myself spinning around to give the bastard a fucking piece of my mind. I stop dead in my tracks, my mouth half open with my retort getting stuck in my throat.

Leaning against the bloody wall is the equivalent of a Greek god made human, who just happens to be my best-friend. Jason's golden hair shines under the streetlight, his hazel eyes lock with mine for a brief second before he bursts out laughing at my ridiculous expression, making my lips lift into a smile as he doubles over.

"You're going to break some hearts tonight Ally." He utters, once his laughter dries up, sauntering over and looking down at me.

"Yeah right." I scoff before linking my arm into his, "more like you will." I mutter, eyeing up his ripped jeans, blue t-shirt and short sleeved shirt that shows off every muscle the boy has.

"Hey," he feigns hurt, clutching his chest as if I'd stabbed him, "I don't break hearts, I mend them." He states so seriously my eyes roll as a giggle escapes me.

Jace was everything I wasn't, good looking, tall, outgoing, charismatic. He always knew just the right words to say to... well everyone, whereas I stumbled and stuttered through almost every conversation.

"You ready for another night on the wrong side of the bar?" Nudging me with his shoulder as we begin walking. I know he's only joking but unlike him I don't have a seemingly unlimited stash of cash. Which is strange as I've lived with him and Mrs Jones for years and they never came across as rich, until we enrolled at uni together.

"Yeah," I sigh as we walk out onto St John street. Shivering I pull my coat tighter around me, my gaze bouncing around the streets as we walk, never staying on one thing for long.

Glancing behind me I freeze. *What's that?* I wonder, staring into the dark trying to focus on a shadow further down the street. Pausing mid-step I stare at the shadow harder, almost pissing myself when Jace's hand grips my shoulder snapping my attention away from the street.

"Ally?" I hear the concern in his voice as I glance back at the shadow I was staring at, sure that it had moved when I'd first looked. Shaking off that weird thought I meet Jace's worried eyes, "You ok?"

I nod not trusting my voice, even as I glance behind me once more. *Where was that shadow again?* I think as I study the now shadow free street. Shivering again I let Jace tug me back into motion, remaining locked in my head until I see the queue waiting for Society to open. Suppressing a groan I give Jace a one-armed hug before leaving him and greeting the bouncers then opening the doors and slipping inside.

Come on Ally, you got this. I remind myself.

"Alyssa," Cindy's voice cuts through the DJ warming up, as she walks briskly toward me, "I thought you were going to bail." She says by way of greeting, as she blows her long blonde fringe from her eyes. Cindy might only be 4ft 9 but for what she lacks in height she makes up for in her no nonsense attitude.

"I wouldn't do that." I assure her, smiling politely as I drop my coat off in the staff room and get my arse behind the bar to help set up.

Rocking back and forth on my aching feet, I try to keep the blood flowing to my toes as I glance at the tiny clock on my till between customers. Four hours down only another five to go, I tell myself as I make up another order of drinks. Society's full to bursting with students and locals alike, all wearing costumes of some degree. Gazing out over the packed dance floor in front of the bar, I watch bodies sway together under the strobe lights. The bright flashes making them appear disjointed and surreal as they dance and I'm taken back to my dreams, so different but also similar.

My skin tingles moments before my eyes lock on him! Dark hair, piercing ice-blue eyes. *No!* My mind screams, *not here, not now!* Closing my eyes I will my sanity to return and when I open them he's gone. Breathing out a relieved sigh I focus on the lass before me as she waves and tries to scream her order at me over the music.

Finding my false smile I lean closer to hear her order of two buckets of woo woo cocktail. Then move on autopilot around the bar mixing two buckets of the red drink with plenty of ice, before accepting the cash payment and nodding as the girl tells me to keep the change.

As my shift goes on with no more psychotic breaks I begin to relax into the familiar rhythm of listening, mixing and taking payments as my shift continues past midnight. Turning to face my next customer a genuine smile lifts my lips as I look at Jace's familiar face.

"How's your night going Ally?" He shouts as I lean over the sticky bar, my nose wrinkling from the alcohol that soaks it.

"The usual," I huff as Jace's smile widens at my discomfort, "what you having?" I ask even though I already know his answer and begin reaching for the bottle fridge behind me. Grabbing a bottle of Corona I turn back, taking the bottle top off and placing it in front of him in time to hear the rest of his order. I take my time mixing the two buckets of cocktail he's ordered before lining up his ten shots of colourful vodka. Turning back to Jace I smile as arms snake around him from behind and his latest fling hugs him tight.

"The tips good tonight?" He asks, smirking at me.

"Yeah rolling in," I joke, holding out my hand, Jace hands me more than enough money to pay for his drinks and detaching his 'friend' so she can carry the two buckets, before retrieving his bottle and the tray of shots from the bar. Ringing up his order, I put the change into my tip glass before turning to the next person waiting to be served, and my heart stops as I forget how to breathe.

Standing before me is my dream man, his dark black fringe falling over one of his ice blue eyes as the other studies me from where he stands, with only the bar separating us. I feel that he can see every secret I've ever buried as his full lips tilt up in the sexiest smirk, straight out of my fantasies. My mind blanks as I run my eyes from his tousled hair, past his perfect cheekbones and jaw. Down across the tight muscles of his chest—barely hidden beneath his thin black shirt—before the bar blocks my view reminding me that I'm at work.

Squeezing my eyes shut, I try to will him back inside my head, where he belongs. But when I open them he's still there. His head tilted to the side—like a bird assessing its prey— as he watches me. "W...what can I get you?" I stammer, as my brain comes back online even as I'm wondering if I've gone completely crazy. *Yeah great Ally talk to the imaginary man, why not.* I chide myself as I wait for his answer.

"You," he answers in a confident tone that makes me shiver.

"W...what?" I ask, sure I've misheard him, I mean I must have. No-one's that blunt, even someone I've created.

"A bottle of Bud." He responds with another smile, as if he knows the effect he's having on me as my cheeks burn. Forcing myself to turn away I mentally berate myself as I open the small fridge and grab a brown bottle. Taking a deep breath I turn back around, expecting him to have disappeared, but he's still there staring at me.

"£3.50" I tell him as I place the bottle before him with shaking hands. With smooth movements he reaches into his back pocket and removes his wallet. Glancing down he selects a note before placing it in my outstretched hand, my skin tingling at the brief contact as his fingertips graze my palm.

"Keep the change." He shouts, making me shiver again at his voice, before he turns and gets swallowed by the crowd. Once he's gone I look down and stare at the crisp twenty pound note I hold, bewildered and confused. I run it through the till and drop the change into my glass. He's real? I question in my head as I try to focus back on my work and fail as I let the other guys take the brunt of the customers. My gaze keeps returning to the crowd, scanning for him as I slowly serve one more drunk customer before I give up and decide to take my break.

The cold water makes me jump as I run my wrists under its flow. *Come on Ally, get it together!* I scream in my head as I try to figure out what's real and what's not. I can feel the panic rising up inside me as I remember his blue eyes watching me. He doesn't exist! I tell myself again, hoping that this time I'll believe myself, but his hand felt so real as it brushed my palm and he gave me real money, I hadn't imagined that. Shaking my head at myself I glance in the mirror once more before returning to the crowded bar and throwing myself back into serving drinks.

The rest of my shift passes in a distracted blur, even Jace realises that my mind is elsewhere on his visits to the bar. All I can think about is Him. The way his voice affected me, the way I almost drooled as my eyes took him in and most importantly the way he was real. I felt his soft fingers as they brushed against my palm leaving behind his money.

I barely notice the crowds leaving as the DJ plays his last song, or the wet cloths I wring out after cleaning down the bar. I'm still not paying attention when I call bye to the rest of the staff outside the club and turn towards home. I've walked over Lendal bridge and I'm nearing York Minster stuck in my head, when a tingle rushes over the nape of my neck. Burrowing into my coat I glance back over my shoulder expecting the street behind me to be empty, but it's not!

Two shadows stop as I do and fear shoots through my whole body as I watch them watching me. Jace's voice fills my head, "...she went missing..." I remember him telling me earlier about a missing student. I'm almost ready to run, when a hand touches my shoulder making me scream and spin around, as the scent of leather and lavender drifts up my nose.

"Are you ok?" His sinfully deep voice makes me jump and shiver in a completely different way as it caresses my ears, and I'm once again rendered momentarily speechless as I stare into his blue eyes.

"Are you real?" I whisper without meaning to, before my cheeks heat and I glance down at the floor mortified.

"I'm very real, I assure you." He responds, his voice both amused and slightly puzzled at the same time. His finger is warm and a little rough as it gently pushes my chin up, forcing me to meet his eyes.

"Who are you?" My mouth blurts out before I can stop it as I stare into his eyes. I know I'm being impolite but I'm struggling to make my brain work like a normal person, obviously.

He opens his mouth to answer but a familiar voice interrupts him, "Ally there you are," Jace calls from down the road. Dream man's eyes flick over my shoulder, tightening slightly before they return to mine and he smiles sadly at me.

"Looks like you already have a knight," he says mockingly before tucking a stray strand of hair behind my ear, "another time maybe Princess." He smirks before turning and walking away.

Gaping like a fish I stare after him long after he's turned the corner and disappeared. "Who was that?" Jace asks, making me jump as he stops next to me.

"I don't know." I whisper, as my heart returns to normal, glancing up at Jace I don't tell him my dream man is most definitely real as I remember the feel of his finger brushing my ear and shiver.

"Huh," Jace mutters before turning back to me, "you heading home?" He asks even though he already knows that I am. Releasing a sigh, I get ready for his arguments about why I should stay out with him instead. "I'll walk you." He says instead, surprising me.

"It's ok Jace, it's not that far." I assure him, not wanting to spoil his night.

"Ally girls are vanishing across the city, of course I'm walking you home." I know he's not joking and won't take no for my answer as he stares down at me, with another sigh I nod and begin walking again.

We walk in silence for a bit before Jace drags me from my thoughts, "You ok, Ally?" He asks, noticing my constant monitoring of the streets.

"Yep." I answer too quickly, making him study me closer.

"You know you're a terrible liar." He states taking my hand and pulling me to a stop, "what's wrong?" I know he won't believe me about my dream man existing, so I focus on something he will believe instead.

"I'm just spooked, I think people were following me." My voice drops to a whisper as I remember the shadowy figures from before. Trembling, I let Jace pull me closer and wrap his arm around me.

"You know I won't let anything bad happen to you don..." He cuts off as we walk into the deserted Minster gardens. Glancing up at him I see that he's standing still, his gaze fixed on something ahead of us. Following his eyes I stare at the empty street.

"Jace?" I question, frowning at him, "what're you looking at?" I ask scanning the empty street again.

He glances down at me once before pushing me away, "Ally run!" He says sternly before pushing me back the way we've come. I stumble back a few steps before rooting my feet and standing my ground.

"Jace? What's going on?" I ask terrified at his unusual behaviour, "there's nothing there," I state before something invisible knocks him backwards. Shaking my head I'm trying to make sense of what I've just seen, when a hand grips my right arm and pulls me sideways.

Screaming I watch as Jace lunges to my right and throws a punch at a...a fucking shadow. I'm still screaming as the shadow lets me go and I stumble backwards. "Ally just run please." Jace screams at me desperately as he blocks me from another shadow man that reaches for me.

I want to run but my feet are stuck, indecision keeping me immobile as I watch Jace fight them. My brain can't make sense of what it's seeing. What are they? How are shadows moving? What's happening to me? My mind screams as I watch. I know I should be helping him but how do you fight shadows? My breath hitches as I watch one of the shadow men grabs Jace around the throat and the other, has he got a knife?

Oh God, not a knife, it's a bloody black sword!

"No!" The word surprises me as it jumps from my throat as the second shadow man pulls its arm back ready to plunge the sword into Jace's belly, drawing all of their attention to me for a second. No, no, no! I keep repeating as my panic spirals higher.

The shadow man returns his attention back to Jace and time slows as the sword moves in a low arc towards his stomach. Suddenly I feel something building inside me as the blade inches closer and closer. Then I'm screaming as I feel something inside my mind break and I close my eyes against the brightest flash of light I've ever seen.

Blinking open my eyes I stare at Jace, his familiar green eyes shine with tears as he watches me back. "Ally?" His voice trembles as he takes a step towards me, but I'm already falling and my eyes are closed before I hit the ground.

Chapter Two

Lysais.

"Is it her?" He demands impatiently as I round the corner, making my frown deepen. I know I should be more careful letting him see how much he gets to me but *I fucking hate this!* I think just as Jacin catches up to Alyssa.

We'd been watching them for a few weeks now and I still couldn't be certain how much Jacin actually remembered. It was now abundantly clear that Alyssa held no memories. Speaking with her tonight had confirmed that suspicion.

A shudder runs through me as I quick squash any feelings of desire as I remember how she'd looked at me with those big, confused blue eyes. *How very clever of the Queen to hide her here, in this pathetic world of base creatures. But was it actually Her?* We'd been misled before. Decoys had been scattered, hidden throughout Agenia, and each one had been utterly convincing. The magic was almost undetectable, the glamour hiding the owner's true image until He'd managed to shatter it.

"It's her!" I snarl as he contemplates some of the bloody ways he'd had to use, to break the powerful magic. *Would she be able to withstand those same methods?* I'm not sure, but I also hope I never have to find out. Not that I have much choice in the matter. "Leave her alone!" I snarl fighting to break free again but he held me on a tighter leash now, since I'd almost managed to break free. Grinning at the small victory, I return my gaze to them and watch as their conversation comes to a halt and they begin making their way towards us.

"I need to test her but how?" He ponders aloud with a sadistic smile, making me wonder just what he has planned for her as I watch her coming closer. I try not to remember how protective she used to get when someone insulted my family and flinched as I realised my mistake. "That's it!" He declared glaring at me with sadistic glee in his blue eyes. "That's the perfect way to draw her magic out if she has any."

Horror consumes me as he summons five Demoran to my side, then laughs as he sends them hunting, with explicit orders to not touch the girl. He watches gleefully from the shadows and I tense as they draw near. Jacin stiffens suddenly, drawing Alyssa's attention to the dangers of the night. A growl breaks loose from my throat as he pushes her behind him, protecting her from our monsters even though they're not there for her, not yet anyway.

Forcing myself to stay still, I watch as Jacin fights to protect the girl—making me more certain she is who we want—is almost painful as I rattle the cage he has me held in, so I can get to her. *Help her!* My heart screams at me. I need to stop this deadly game he's set in motion. Stifling my fears I focus on the battle before us, noting how Jacin moves to block each Demoran. Glancing quickly to my left I sneer at the pleasure I see in his eyes as one draws its shadow blade back, poised to attack her protector, until a scream drags our attention back to the fight.

"No!" She screams, making everyone pause and stare at her. As fury flares briefly in her eyes we can finally feel it. Her magic is rising, building, wanting to break free from whatever binds are holding it dormant. Her skin begins to glow and her eyes close before it explodes out, lighting up the dark park and banishing our Demoran.

It's delicious and ferocious as it burns them away leaving only her and Jacin in the park, "vicious" he growls in pleasure as we both watch her power flare. It lasts only a moment but it solidifies his plans. "I must bring her home! The King will be so pleased with me." He snarls, making me shudder as I imagine what my Father would do to her. I could almost hear the approval he needed reflected in his words, watching the girl go limp. She nearly hits the floor before a stunned Jacin jolts forward and catches her.

What had kept her hidden? And what was binding her magic? It had been driving me mad since we'd first found her. She looked and acted completely human, the glamour was strong, stronger than the other decoys. I couldn't detect it at all, so I didn't want to imagine what it was going to take to break it?

Frustrated I watch Jacin gently pick her up before walking away into the night bristling at not being able to hold her that close myself. It should be me, not him, I sneer in my head, wanting to be closer to her.

"Oh how we're going to break her little brother," his murmur draw my attention back to him as I try to glean his thoughts through the bond they forced on me.

She'll never trust you, she'll see right through your bullshit. I snarl inside my head, knowing he'll hear me as he turns away from the park.

"Oh she might not trust me, but she trusted you once before, I'm sure she'll grow to trust you again especially with that pesky bond you have with her." He drawls his explanation slowly, lazily, as if I'm too dumb to understand, before grabbing the shadows closest to us and forcing me to follow.

Chapter Three

Alyssa.

Ducking between dancers, colours are nothing but a blur, before I exit through the closest archway. Into one of the many gardens. Dashing through the flowerbeds, gilded silver by the moonlight, I escape further into the dark. I'm almost in the clear when a hand closes around my arm, yanking me backwards. Fear races through me as I settle against a warm body and a rough hand covers my mouth before any scream can escape.

"Hush. Ally it's me, it's Jacin." His warm voice brushes across my ear, calming my racing heart rate as I relax against his hard body.

"What are you doing out here?" I whisper when he frees my mouth.

"Hiding," Jacin states as I turn to face him, grinning at his cheeky smile. His long almost white hair shines silver in the moonlight, it's pulled back from his face showing off his slightly pointed ears. I like them even if he doesn't, they make him different. They're smaller than the rest of ours, more like an elf than fairy.

Searching his strange golden eyes as they gleam down at me, I can't help but wonder why he's hiding out here. "From what?" I ask bewildered. Jacin's popular with everyone in the palace, from servants to lords, and definitely with the ladies. So why is he hiding out here?

"Not what Ally, but who." He states before pausing to drive me crazy. He continues with a mischievous smirk, "I've escaped from the attentions of Lady Blossom who is obsessed with matching me up with her eldest daughter." His face twists with a grimace as he finishes his explanation .

"Lady Lily isn't that bad," I say gently, sympathising both with Jacin and Lady Blossom.

"Not that bad? She's a typical Spring Court Lady, full of volatile politeness that would kill me." He jokes, smiling as I shake my head at him before continuing, "you know me Ally, I like my freedom, could you really see me as the Lord of Spring?" He asks dead *seriously.*

I take a moment trying to imagine Jacin being polite, sitting and listening to the people's problems in the spring court, without cracking a joke. I end up laughing while shaking my head. "No Jacin I don't think the spring court is the place for you."

"Too right! My place is by your side." He says, bopping me on the nose with his finger before turning his jovial gaze on me, "And what are you doing running around the gardens?"

"Escaping as well, you know how much I love attending these events, and..." I trail off before I let him know my disappointment that Ly had to go home before the spring equinox ball. I know nobody likes Lysias, due to his father being evil incarnate. Not that I've met the Shadow King of course, but even Ly hates his father, so he must be evil right?

"And Lysias isn't here." Jacin finishes for me, bringing me back from my spiraling thoughts. But even if he doesn't say anything bad he can't quite hide his disapproving tone.

"He isn't that bad, Jacin..." I begin to defend Ly as Jacin interrupts, his voice firm.

"I know you think so but he isn't to be trusted."

Shaking my head I step away from him, taking a deep breath as I look out over the gardens. Fighting not to lose my temper with my friend. "Ally!" Jacin's scream is the only warning I get before I'm lifted off my feet and thrown across the manicured lawn.

I jolt awake, shivering in the breeze from my open window. *It was only a dream,* I remind myself even as my brow furrows, and I have to pry my fingers from my mattress. The sensation of falling is etched in my body as I try to calm my racing heart. Reluctantly thinking back on the dream, from before I was thrown, I don't want to analyse what I'd seen. *Why was Jace there? It's my imaginary world, so why on earth was I dreaming about him? He'd never been in my dreams before. And why the hell did he look so strange?* I think as I untangle myself from my sheets.

I wonder where I get the inspiration for my strange dreams. It's almost as if my subconscious is trying to tell me something.

Something strange and fantastical, something beyond belief. Shaking my head I remind myself that *the dreams mean nothing, they're a coping mechanism* I repeat in my head, trying to dispel my confusion. *Maybe it's because he's the only friend you have,* my mind tells me sarcastically. But what about my dream man, is he real or imagined?

Replaying last night's encounter with him once more, I find myself smiling as I allow myself to wonder if he is real—I'm still not 100% convinced that he is—will I meet him again? Or maybe I've finally snapped and my dreams have now morphed into hallucinations, very real hallucinations that are taking on a solid shape.

More confused than ever I laugh at the absurdity that is my life. Glancing around my dorm room, my mind turning over last night again and again, I swallow a scream as I realise something important.

I can't remember how I got back here. I try forcing myself to retrace my steps back here—I know the route I must have taken —but searching my memory of last night reveals nothing!

I remember meeting Him, and I remember Jace meeting me, but no matter how hard I try I can't remember walking home. Scrunching up my face, as panic begins to shorten my breath and my chest feels like it's trapped in a vice. I look around my room thinking, hoping, it will somehow answer my questions. But everything looks the same; my desk is still neatly organised, my cat posters are still on the plain walls. So why do I feel like something's missing?

There's a gap in my memory that I just can't figure out. Huffing in annoyance, I grab my phone from beneath my pillow and groan at the amount of missed calls. 36! *What the hell happened last night?* I wonder as I unlock it and look at the two names, repeated again and again. Jace and Mrs Jones.

Oh, man I'm so dead, I think to myself stealing a glance at the small clock in the corner of my phone screen and cringing. It's already 8 o'clock. *Crap!* I'm going to be late I realise, even as I throw myself off my bed and spring into action. I need to get ready, FAST! I'm meant to be meeting Jace before my lecture. Praying that the bathroom's empty, I shove my feet into my favourite slippers, grab clean clothes from my wardrobe without checking they match, and quietly let myself out into the hall, before sprinting to the communal bathroom.

I don't bump into anyone before slipping into the thankfully empty bathroom. After the quickest shower of my life, I'm wiping the steam from the mirror to quickly study my face as my phone begins vibrating urgently on the side. *God, I look tired*, I grimace studying the bags under my eyes that weren't there yesterday.

Maybe I'm working too much? I think briefly before shrugging at myself and smiling at the mirror and leaving the bathroom. Grabbing my bag, I shake my head at myself for being so strange, locking the flat door then sprinting down the stairs to meet Jace.

It's been a month since we'd left what had been home for the last year to come study at York St John University. I smile as I remember Lilah's face when we'd told her we were going to move out. I still don't know if she was happy or sad with our decision, but she'd supported us either way.

Over those four weeks I'd got my routine running like clockwork. From waking up before any of my so-called 'flat-mates,' to drinking my coffee alone in our communal living room—if you could call it that—watching the sky lighten from indigo, to pink to orange to light blue. Dawn's my favourite time of the day, calming me no matter how stressed my eventful dreams made me feel.

At nine on the dot I'm normally walking out of the front door with my overfull book bag to meet a smiling Jace, as he waits for me, to go for my second coffee of the day and sometimes a sinfully sugary treat too!

Swinging open the bottom door I smile as I hear his voice, "Good morning Ally," he greets me, then glances down at his watch. His playful smirk at my predictability morphs to confusion as he notes the time, "you're late?" He accuses questioningly staring at me intently.

"Hey Jace," I respond with forced brightness, refusing to acknowledge that I of all people am running late.

"What happened last night?" I ask a slight tremor in my voice as I watch his face carefully.

"What do you mean?"

"I can't remember getting home?"

"Maybe someone slipped something into your drink?" He explains reasonably but who would do that? None of my colleagues at Society surely.

"Then what's with all the missed calls?" I ask back, catching him off guard a moment as his eyebrows shoot up.

"Well I kinda panicked when you weren't behind the bar at Society, and when you didn't answer your phone I called Lilah." He explains sheepishly as my brows furrow. "With everything going in this city I was worried Ally, but then Cindy said weren't feeling well and had gone home, so..."

"So you came looking for me." I fill in the rest of his sentence. I thought about it all and realised maybe that's why I'd seen Dream man and why he'd felt so real, but why would someone I work with spike my drink?

"Yeah," Jace answers seeing me working things out in my head, "Gothic lecture?" He asks changing the subject, even though he already knows my answer.

I'm a creature of habit and rarely do I venture off my plotted path. *Except for last night.* I cringe as the thought crosses my mind, "Yep." I answer, smiling up at him as we walk the short distance between my dorm and the coffee counter en route to my lecture hall in Fountains.

"So how come you didn't get me to walk home last night?" He asks, his voice dropping a little as we wait in line for coffee.

"I just wanted to get home." I answer honestly, not mentioning talking to a hallucination, I thought was real, he didn't need to know my mental state was fluctuating again.

"But on your own?" I look at him as he continues to question me, for a moment I'm almost sure I see something in his eyes. But he blinks and it's gone before I can really register what I think I've seen.

"Yes!" I bite back defensively. "I am a grown woman, you know."

"Woah" he exclaims, throwing his hands up in defense, "I just worry about you Ally, I guess you've not heard about Trisha then?" He continues gently.

"No," I answered confused, "Trisha, who?" Jason's a complete socialite and always surrounded by endless hordes of women I don't know.

"Trisha Goodwin." When I still show no sign of recognition he continues. "She's gone missing." He mumbles, gaining my undivided attention, and finally pulling my mind away from the confusing spirals of my mystery man, missing time and mystifying dreams.

She's the fourth woman to vanish this term, with the third still missing and the first two found dead. Found floating in the river by police, completely drained of blood. It was so strange and the police had no leads, and no evidence. "Oh no." I murmured in shock, scared for the girl—Trisha—I corrected myself sternly, even if I didn't know her, "I hope she's found safe." I mumble.

"Me too." Jason agrees as we move up to the counter, "one caramel latte and an espresso, to go please." Jason orders for the both of us. As I gaze longingly at the selection of brownies arranged temptingly on the counter, I sink my teeth into my lip to stop myself from adding one to our order. Today is not quite a sugary treat day...not yet anyway.

"£8.60 please." The lass behind the counter asked, drawing my attention away from the unhealthy, sinfully delicious snacks. She's smiling at Jason like he's God's gift to women, making me sigh in resignation as I wait for the flirting to begin. Shaking my head, I turned to the plate glass window that looks out onto the busy street, and began watching people as we waited for our drinks. Scanning the faces of students and teachers as they pass I feel my blood run cold. There he is!

My dream man!

He looks as real as he did last night in the club, but could he be real? I definitely don't feel like I'm on drugs, but how can he be real? Even now the shadows seem alive shifting around him. His blue eyes are locked on me, watching me back as I study him. Sucking in a breath, I can't believe what I'm seeing. My delusions have definitely taken a turn for the worst. I'm no longer just dreaming of this strange, beautiful man. I'm now seeing him in my waking hours too. *He might be real.* My traitorous mind whispers as it tugs how real he felt last night to the fore front of my mind. Unable to look away I notice that no one walks near him, or even looks at him. It's like he's not even there, making me laugh at myself for considering he could be real.

I hear Jason shouting my name but ignore him. Just like in my dreams I feel drawn towards my mystery man, my shadow prince and my body acts on instinct, before my rational mind can catch up. I'm walking to him. I barely register leaving the café and pushing open the front doors that lead to the busy street. Or pushing past the incoming students, making them grumble as they stream around me, deep in their own morning routines and oblivious to my plight. My desperate need to find out if he's real, who he is and why I dream about him outshines any common sense. *Please be real, please be real,* my mind is repeating as I stumble out of a group of students and into the rare November sunshine, but he's gone!

No! No! No! I scream in my head as I search the path where he'd been standing only moments ago.

"Ally!" I turn to Jason's panicked eyes as he searches mine, "what's wrong?" He asks handing me my latte.

"I saw him." I whisper still not able to believe that he'd been real.

"Who?"

"Him Jason! The shadow man from my dreams." His face pales slightly and his eyes crinkle a little as he looks at me with eyes full of sympathy.

"He's not real Ally." He says patiently, "you know that right?" He says rationally.

"Yes, no. Urgh, I don't know Jace?" I answer, squeezing my eyes shut. I count to ten, before telling Jace what he wants to hear, "of course I know that," but I can't shake the feeling that he is real, and had been standing right there watching me. "I must be crazy." I mumble.

"You are not crazy." Gripping my hand tightly, Jace sounds angry as he reassures me for the umpteenth time since we met three years ago. Jason had found me all those years ago, and he hadn't left my side since. "You went through something tragic Ally." He says, making me smile into his brown eyes, as I nod and let him pull me back towards uni. I must sound like a broken record to him by now, and I honestly don't know why he sticks by me.

I take one last look over my shoulder, but he's not there. Shaking my head, I give Jace's hand a squeeze before letting it go, and follow him though the doors, into the crowded hallway outside the room where my lecture is due to start soon. "See you after?" I question Jace as the tutor arrives to open the lecture hall.

"Of course." He smiles, tucking a loose strand of my hair behind my ear before turning to leave, "go be a bookworm." He chucks back at me over his shoulder before he's swallowed up by the English Lit students, making me smile as I walk inside and find a seat.

The lecture is all about the vampire myth. It's interesting, but my mind keeps returning to my Shadow Prince. *My Shadow Prince? Where did that thought come from? He isn't mine! He isn't even real.* I'm still trying to rid my brain of him and focus on the tutor when my phone vibrates in my pocket. Slowly reaching down to dig it out without drawing attention to myself, I steal a glance at the sender name. It's Cindy, my boss. Sighing I open up her message: *Heya Ally, can you work this evening? X*

I know I should say no, Jace wanted me to come clubbing tonight but an extra shift would mean more money. Instead, I type back. *Sure no problem.*

My leg bounces as I wait for her reply, *Great, you start at 6pm X*

She signs every message with a kiss, making me chuckle and

shake my head every time she messages. She's like 60 odd, and still trying to 'fit in with the kids', as she calls us.

Looking back up at the slide show I try to pick up where I'd left off, but knew it was hopeless as I listened to my tutor without hearing any of her words. I'm just about to look back down at my phone and message Jace, when I see my dream man again.

He's peering in through the window in the door, staring straight at me. I smile without meaning to as I stare into his beautiful, inhuman eyes. He's just like my dream...perfect. I bite my bottom lip whilst trying to decide if I should throw caution to the wind, and try to interact with my delusion.

I'm leaning forward in my seat, but I don't care. All I want to do is run from this room and throw myself into his arms. I can feel the longing settle deep in my heart as we continue to stare at each other. I feel that same pull now as I do in my dreams, tugging me towards him. My heart is racing, and I'm biting my lip harder when I make up my mind and meet his eyes again. What the hell if he is a delusion then he's a sexy as hell illusion and *if I am crazy then I might as well enjoy it*, I think throwing caution to the wind.

Who are you? I mouth at him, making his full, kissable lips turn up at the sides for an instant, then his perfect blue eyes fill with sadness and the shadows around him intensify, hiding him from view. He's gone again.

Well it's official, you've completely lost it Ally! I berate myself, whilst shaking my head. I wait out the rest of the lecture staring at the door, hoping he'll return and answer my question, paying absolutely no attention to the room around me.

Does he know me from before? I think, before cursing myself silently for being so stupid. *There is no such thing as otherworldly creatures, with swirling shadows!* I let out an imaginary scream clinging desperately to reality and looked down at my phone to WhatsApp Jace.

So I'm crackers. I send.

Why? He responds in record time.

I've seen him again.

Ally, have you taken your Meds today? He's only half joking with his response.

Maybe not. I respond honestly, I've never told a lie—that I know of—in the last three years. It's why I still have to see a therapist, and why they still prescribe me anti-psychotic medication.

Bloody hell, you know you need them! His short response pings through quickly, but his WhatsApp status tells me he's typing again so I wait. *Why haven't you taken them? How long have you been off them?*

They make me feel funny, disconnected. I respond knowing he's going to go mental at me.

We'll talk about it when you get out. I can hear his strict tone in my head as I read his response and know there's no room for argument. Jace is as over-protective of me as a big brother would be, but I hate taking those stupid pills and if the only downside is me seeing a sexy man then so be it. I'm fine with that.

Smiling to myself, I wait for everyone to file out of the lecture hall before making my way to the front to ask Dr Lisa Smith if today's lecture slides will be on Moodle later. I'm stalling before meeting up with Jace, knowing exactly what he's going to say to me, and who will be waiting on the other end of his phone.

Lisa's looking at me expectantly, and I startle, realising I've been staring at her as if I had something further to ask. I don't. "Is everything ok Alyssa?" She asks kindly when I still don't speak.

"Erm, yes thanks." I reply reluctantly, knowing my time's up and I'll have to face the music, "see you next time." I say hitching my bag strap onto my shoulder and heading for the door.

"Alyssa Jones!" Jace scolds me as I push it open and almost walk into his chest.

"Not here." I mutter, holding up my hand to stop his tirade, as I hear Mrs Jones' shrill tone come from his phone speaker. Lilah, my adoptive mum was awesome, always treating me the same as Jace. She'd helped me re-learn how to read, write, and do sums until eventually I passed my G.C.S.E exams at home alongside Jace. She even encouraged me through college, until here I was at York St John University, following my passion for reading as I study English Literature. She had always supported my decisions, except when it came to taking my damn pills. "Pass her here," I sigh, holding out my hand.

"Alyssa, what are you thinking?" Lilah demands before I even get the phone up to my ear.

"That I'm nineteen years old and don't want to take the damn pills." I'm walking as I talk trying to get away from anyone that could be in my English seminars.

"Do not give me that!" She almost screams down the phone, "you know you need them."

"But they make me feel odd Lilah, like I'm disconnected from everything." I try to explain yet again.

"They're supposed to Sweetie." She tries to console me, using her sympathetic voice.

"No, I want to feel things." I'm determined to win this round, "I'm a grown woman, for goodness' sake. I can make my own decisions." I'm getting angry now, but I can't help it. When I don't take the pills I feel like I'm connected to everything around me, like I'm actually alive. The only downside is the hallucinations and mad dreams.

"If that's the way you feel then fine, do what you want." She says patiently, making me feel bad instantly, "put Jace back on the phone please." And that's it. She's done with me for now. Shaking my head, I pass the phone back and storm off towards my dorm block, glancing back once to make sure Jace is following. He's a few steps behind so I can't hear what he's saying to his mum, but he looks pale and slightly frightened when he meets my eyes. I watch him nod once, before putting his phone away and striding to catch up to me, his long legs quickly closing the distance between us.

"Don't you even start!" I mumble at him when he opens his mouth, He closes it without making a sound, and reconsiders what he was about to say.

"Are we still on for tonight?" He asks, trying to cool my temper down.

I look at him quizzically then remember. Shit. I haven't told him I'm working tonight.

"Sorry Jace but I've got work. Maybe at the weekend?" I try to sound sorry but I'm still too angry with him. Furious that he once again called his mum on me.

"Come on Ally!" He exclaims, clearly frustrated, "that's what you always say."

"I know, I'm sorry. Friday ok?"

"Promise?"

"I promise." I agree bumping his shoulder.

"And no more talk of the shadow man?" He asks carefully.

"Fine." I stumble over the word, before leaving him on the path and going inside. I need to read another one of my core texts for this module.

I know he's hiding something from me, but what it is I've never been able to figure out. Shaking my head I walk up the two flights of stairs, down the hallway, and let myself into my dorm room. Walking straight to the window, I look down at Jace's face and wave as he waits outside. He's frowning a little as he waves back before turning and walking down the path towards his own dorm room. *What's his problem?* I think to myself before drifting away and surveying the small communal living room. It's depressing really with the dull beige walls, a small TV on its white built-in stand, and the sad looking sofa which has seen one too many bums.

Sighing, I settle in on the sofa, grab my books from my bag and dive back into the world of Bram Stoker's Dracula. Wielding my favourite pen and highlighter, I set to work marking anything that could be of interest as I read. Despite the captivating text, half an hour later I'm still staring at the first page, my thoughts consumed with my dream man instead of Dracula. I can see him, framed by the small window of the door, his dark brooding eyes set above chiseled cheek bones. I can feel my blood warming, just thinking about the hottie I've imagined.

I'm smiling to myself as I walk to the kitchen deciding that a cup of coffee might help me concentrate on the words of my book. Glancing at the clock on the wall, I see that I still have hours before my shift at Society. That gives me plenty of time to study my first core text of the semester. Following the soothing motions of making myself a cuppa, I let my heated thoughts calm down, until I can finally push Him from my thoughts. With my favourite Nightmare Before Christmas mug warming my hands, I settle back down on the sofa and delve into Dracula's story.

I'm about a quarter of the way through the book when my alarm makes me jump, reluctantly reminding me that I need to get ready for work.

Chapter Four

Jacin

For Fucksake, I think to myself as I leave Alyssa's dorm. We'd been sent here to keep her safe. From where and from what was a little foggy, it always had been. Lilah knew more about what we were doing, and where we came from, but she'd refused to tell me in case I let it slip to Ally.

Speaking to Ally this morning had reassured me a little, I'd been secretly relieved that she didn't remember the antics from last night. *How the hell was I supposed to explain away the shadow warriors? And the damn magic,* I was desperately clinging to the hope that that would be an isolated incident. However, something told me I was clutching at straws wishing that. Sighing, I walk off towards my own dorm, once again cursing the fact that we'd been housed so far from each other, it would be easier to keep her safe if we lived together but I'd have to make do.

My memory might be spotty, but I know how I feel for her and it's never changed over the last three years. I needed to keep her safe. I pulled out my phone and dialled Lilah back.

"She's fuming you know," I explain as I push open the door to my building.

"That's to be expected, Dear." Lilah calmly explains, then catches me off guard by asking, "is he really there?"

"I've not seen Him, but Ally's certain that she has and I'm inclined to believe her. She's never hallucinated that vividly before."

"You need to come home," Lilah demands, before thinking it through properly, her protective instincts flaring.

"And how would I explain that to her; hey Ally sorry but mum wants us back home for no apparent reason. Yeah, that would go down well." I laugh down the phone.

"I suppose so." She says sceptically, "she must not interact with him Jacin. It's not safe." She stresses.

"Why can't we just tell her or go home?" I ask in frustration for what must have been the thousandth time.

"We can't, not yet. Ally isn't ready."

I know Lilah's right, the mental block on Ally would shred her mind to pieces if triggered. Fuck knows why that safety measure was put into place, but whatever the reason, it scared the hell out of me.

I'd worked hard to ensure I'd never come close to triggering it. "I'll keep her safe, Lilah." I muttered, wondering how exactly I would achieve that, and shoved my way into my empty dorm. If Ally was right, and the Shadow son-of-a-bitch really was here, it made our job a heck of a lot harder. Three years. We'd only made it three short years, before he managed to figure out where we were hidden.

Raging, I felt the skin of my knuckles split open as they connected with the wall of my small bedroom. *Why couldn't he have just left her alone?*

The rest of my day passed with me running through different scenarios in my head, each less likely to succeed than the one before. Perhaps I could force Ally to change universities? Nah she wouldn't do that, she liked it too much here in York. Maybe I could use the recent disappearances and murders? Or maybe I could force Him to leave her alone? Yeah right! I laugh at myself even thinking that.

I didn't know what his game was, but something inside me screamed at letting him near her. There was a deep distrust when it came to Ally's dream man. All I know is that we'd be staying put for now. That meant Ally had another shift at Society tonight, and I was damn well going to protect her!

Chapter Five

Alyssa.

My head is pounding as I walk into Society to start my extra shift, and I'm already regretting taking it on. It's Wednesday night. Student night, and Society's packed as usual. My head gives another dull throb, in time to the music, as I serve a group of students. And I find myself wishing again that I was in my dorm, wrapped up in bed with a good book instead. I've still got four hours of my shift left, and I stare out at the students, watching as they dance or order drinks.

I serve yet another drunk lass before sighing, and searching the club once more. He's not here. I know he's not, but I can't keep myself from looking for his blue eyes and dark hair.

"Alyssa!" Cindy's voice breaks through to me.

"Yeah?" I call back, competing with the music.

"I need you to do a glass run." Her eyes plead with me, even though she knows I hate leaving the bar.

"Fine." I agree, rubbing my head and grabbing an empty glass collector from near the sink, before brushing past her.

My already bad mood sours further, with each grope that my arse receives as I push past drunk people, stooping to pick up empty or discarded glasses around the dance floor. I'm just about to scream at another guy, whose uninvited hand has found me, when a deep growl reverberates through the room.

Glancing up, I meet ice blue eyes that are full of fury, all directed at the punk behind me. "Leave!" He growls at him, before shifting his focus to me. Bending towards me. I stop breathing as his face brushes my cheek, "Hey Princess." He breathes into my ear, making me shiver. He must be real. His breath against my ear feels pretty real.

"Who are you?" I ask, knowing that somehow he can hear me over the music, without me raising my voice. His smile confirms it.

"Dance with me?" He asks, holding out his hand like a gentleman.

Opening my mouth to respond, I scream in shock. Ice cold liquid soaks through the back of my thin shirt. Spinning around, I glare at the girl standing behind me with a stunned look on her face and a now empty glass in her hand. Backing away from me, she begins apologising, but I can't hear her words as a drum and bass track drowns her out.

Tonight is so not my night, I think before I remember Mister tall, dark and handsome standing behind me. Groaning, I turn slowly to face him. He's smirking! Anger rises inside me as I stare at his smirk. He's my dream man. I created him. He should not be enjoying my bad luck. Sticking up my middle finger, I turn and stalk off back to the bar, my eyes hunting for Cindy.

Dumping my half full tray near the glass washer, I search for Luke the bar manager instead. Catching his eye; I mouth, 'where's Cindy?' Before following his pointed finger to the cellar door. Closing my eyes, and trying to tamp down on my anger, my hand slaps against the door to push it open.

"Cindy?" I call out on my way downstairs.

"Alyssa?" She asks from somewhere below.

"I need to go home." I respond as my foot hits the concrete floor, and she pops her head around a shelf of bottles.

"What?" She says and I can read the disbelief in her eyes, I've never left a shift early.

"I'm not feeling well." I grumble as she walks towards me.

"But we'll be a person short." She argues, thinking only of her profits, rather than the welfare of her staff.

"I think I might throw up." I plead, knowing that the food hygiene law will stop me from being able to work. Her face crumples into a frown as she scrutinises my face, but I know I've won before she answers.

"You do look a little pale." Nodding, I pull my sticky shirt away from my back as I wait for her to say the words. "Ok hun, go home. I hope you feel better soon." I'm just about to turn when her concerned voice stops me, to ask "When's your next shift?"

"Saturday." I mumble.

"Ok, if you're still not well, let me know so I can cover it." Then she turns back to her clipboard and continues taking inventory, dismissing me. I try not to run up the stairs as my wet skirt slaps the back of my thighs. Waving to Luke on my way past, I duck into the small staff area, to retrieve my coat and phone from my locker. Then I'm heading for the back door that reads emergency exit.

Massaging my temples, I lean against the brick wall in the thin alley behind Society, willing my headache to go away. I'm not looking forward to my walk home, as the cool night air hits my soaked clothes and bare skin. But, I refuse to get a taxi and waste money. Sucking in a deep breath I turn toward the crowded street, and slip my arms into my warm coat.

My boots make a familiar dull thud on the pavement, as I dodge drunk students and their garbled catcalls. Keeping my head down, I'm walking past Society's busy entrance, and turning the corner onto Lendal bridge when I hear a high-pitched scream.

Without thinking, I run back around the corner, past the new Aviva building. I spot the woman standing under the bridge, as a man stalks towards her. She looks to be my own age, with long dirty blonde hair that whips around her face in the wind blowing off of the river.

"My, my, all alone little witch." The man laughs at the terrified woman as he takes another step in her direction.

"I'm not a witch," she screams, her voice wavering only slightly, "please leave me alone."

"Oh but you are," he drawls, "and I bet you taste just as sweet as the ones I've already tasted." As he speaks, I draw close enough to see a flash of white against his lips. *Fangs?* I think I'm confused.

I'm just about to open my mouth, to scream and distract the man, when she throws out her hands towards him. My scream sticks in my throat and I blink. Absolutely certain I'm having another hallucination, as I watch a bright blue blast come from her hands, hitting the man in his chest and pushing him back towards the river.

Rubbing my eyes, I call out as someone pushes me aside and I fall, scrapping my hands on the hard floor. Ignoring the stinging pain, my eyes return to the woman under the bridge. Now there's another woman standing in front of the first. *Where the hell did she come from?* She has short dark hair that neatly frames her serious looking face. *That must be who pushed me,* my mind supplies as I watch her pull a long, wicked looking sword from a sheath on her back. *What am I seeing?* I think bewildered at how my life seems to have become a story from a book.

The first lass is staring at her hands in disbelief as she shakes them, clearing them of the blue bands of light that run between her fingers, and shaking her head. Pushing myself up from the floor—instead of away from this insanity—I run to where she's standing.

"You ok?" I ask, ignoring the strange man and the woman with the sword. She nods at me, before returning her focus to the man. Following her, I finally get a good look at his face; his eyes are blood-red, his skin has a slightly blue tint to it and or those fangs? Yep, He definitely has fangs protruding from his mouth as he sneers at the dark haired women. It's like he has stepped out of Bram Stoker's Dracula.

"I'm going to kill you." The other woman snarls threateningly at him.

"Good little huntress, always following orders." He mocks at her, with an evil smile, before turning his gaze towards me. "And what have we here?" He asks, his red gaze honing in on me as he sniffs the air. *What a weirdo,* my mind supplies. I watch astounded, as he draws in another lungful of night air. Almost as if he can smell me from where he stands.

You've fully lost it now Ally, I tell myself as I try to explain to myself how he doesn't seem to be human. I come up blank. Glancing between the other two women, I know I can't have imagined him, as they can clearly see him too. *What the hell is going on?* I silently question.

"Run, both of you." The dark haired woman hisses, without

looking away from the man, vampire, thing- whatever he is. Without thinking twice, I grab the woman's hand and run, forcing her to follow me.

"My master will put you all in your rightful places." The vampire calls after us as we flee, and the woman—the huntress my confused mind supplies—stays behind guarding our backs.

My lungs are killing from sucking in the frigid air as we run across Lendal Bridge, back towards the bright lights of the city centre. We've just made it to the Minster when I hear footsteps behind us. Terrified, I glance over my shoulder, then sigh with relief as the other woman closes the distance between us faster than humanly possible. One minute she's at least fifteen steps away from us and then, as I blink, she's standing in front of the other woman, running her hands over her.

"What are you?" I ask, knowing I'm staring at her.

Turning towards me, she pins me with her dark brown eyes. "Thank you." She says, giving me a glimpse of fangs before turning back to the shaking woman besides me. "Charleene, what happened?" She asks her tone, showing a hint of concern.

"I...He..." She trails off clearly not knowing what to say, or questioning the fact that the woman before her has fangs and can move in the blink of an eye. I know I am. Suddenly my fear makes itself known, and I begin rattling off questions.

"What are you?" I repeat, "what was that man? How are you real?" My questions draw the woman's gaze again as she sighs in frustration. Pinning me in place with a stern gaze, she walks over to me and grabs my chin in a bruising grip.

"You saw nothing. You walked home alone and nothing strange happened." She says commandingly, staring into my eyes. I feel my mind fogging over as her words begin to bury themselves in it.

My headache returns with a vengeance as the pain intensifies, clearing away the foggy feeling. My hands grip my head. It feels like my mind is splitting in two as the woman's words fight to remain in it. "GET AWAY FROM ME!" I scream, as the pain swallows me and I feel a pop inside my mind.

Suddenly I'm no longer standing in the street, but in a large room that sparkles in sudden sunshine. Glancing around, I struggle to place where I am. It was night a second ago? I find Jace standing next to me, dressed in a black fitted suit, with delicate silver swirls on the cuffs and around the silver buttons. Confused, a man's voice draws my attention away, and I find myself staring into a pair of vivid green eyes.

"Red, blue, bronze and green, magic I bind remain unseen..." His voice is familiar as are his tears filled eyes, but I don't know how I know him.

Then I'm back in front of the minister, staring into dark brown eyes with a silver ring around the pupil. My lips pull up in a snarl and I feel pleased as those strange eyes widen in surprise. Suddenly, she's flung away from me on an invisible wind.

"What are you?" She snarls at me before sniffing the air, like the man-thing did back below the bridge. She's about to say something else, when her eyes lock onto something behind me.

No, not something. Someone. I realise, as a deep familiar voice filled with barely contained anger rumbles over my shoulder. "I suggest you leave, while you still can Huntress," I shiver as my dream man's voice caresses my ears, calming the raging storm that's building inside my head again, "and take your pet with you."

I watch as what-ever-she-is takes a step back in fear and her eyes widen in confusion. "Impossible," she throws at us, "you're kind don't..."

She breaks off mid-sentence as he steps up behind me, "Leave now." He snarls, before I feel his arms close around me. One arm around my back, while the other settles behind my legs. My eyes close as the world swings, opening them again only as my head settles comfortably against his warm shoulder. I feel as though a fire is burning through my head, but I force myself to look into his eyes as a memory surfaces.

"Lysias." I whisper, smiling weakly before closing my eyes again and letting the darkness take my pain away.

"You're safe now princess." He says into my hair just before I lose consciousness.

The darkness only lasts for a few seconds, before I find myself back in the large room. Looking around I find Jace standing next to me again, staring at me in concern. "It's going to be ok Ally." He says, trying to reassure me.

Nodding I reach up, and wipe the tears from my cheeks. I'm not allowed to cry, not allowed to look weak, I remind myself. But I can feel that my heart is broken, shattered into a thousand pieces.

A door slams shut, and my gaze flicks up to see a couple walking towards me. The man has kind green eyes that seem to shine, his white hair has been braided at the sides, like Jacin's. That's strange? I think. Father always wears his hair down, only warriors braid their hair.

My mother—I don't know how I know that's who she is but I do— sobs next to him, drawing my eyes to hers.   They're a deep shade of violet, set into a beautiful face that looks like mine will when I'm older. I see they're both crying, as they close the distance. I'm about to ask what's going on, but my father's voice stops me, "it must be done, she must be kept safe." He says to mother, as he wraps an arm around her shaking shoulders."

"What must be done?" I question, fear breaking through my pain.

"Forgive us?" He pleads, locking his eyes with mine.

Glancing around I find Jace standing next to me. Then father's voice forces my attention back to him. I'm crying again as I look into his familiar green eyes as his own tears spill over his cheeks but his voice is strong as he begins a spell. "Red, blue, bronze and green, magic I bind remain unseen, hide our daughter from His sight, until her power burns too bright..."

"No," I try to interrupt as I feel the magic taking hold inside my mind, forcing me to forget, but father continues.

"Yellow, brown, silver, pink, give my daughter time to think, as He searches high and low, steady times rushing flow..."

I'm shaking my head now, trying to stop what he's weaving. He opens his mouth to speak again but something rips me from my dream before I can hear his words.

"Get your hands off of her!" Jace's angry snarl rips me from the dream, and my eyes flash open.

Where am I? I wonder, Why am I floating? No, not floating. I'm being carried I realise as I feel his strong arms around me. Confused, I look up at my very real dream man, before following his gaze to find that we're standing outside my dorm building. With a very angry Jace standing in front of the doors. His face is livid as he stares at me. No, not at me.

He's staring at my dream man, he sees him too! I'm too shocked to speak as the reality of my situation dawns on me. Jace is angrier than I've ever seen him, and as I look back up at my dream man I'm shocked to see shadows dancing around his head.

Closing my eyes and shaking my head, I wonder if I hit it, and then I realise I can't remember anything after leaving the alley behind Society. Panic thunders through my body, making it shake as I try to force myself to remember.

"What's happening?" I question in a shaky voice, "how did I get here?" I ask as Jace's voice drowns mine out.

"Put her down, I will not tell you again!" Jace spits out, his hands balling into fists.

"I'm not here to fight you half-breed." Dream man snarls before turning his inhuman gaze to me, his tone softens, "I'm making sure she's safe." His voice makes me shiver and I feel a jolt of desire course through me.

"Like hell you are." Jace retorts.

"Both of you stop it!" I shout silencing whatever dream man was about to say. "Please put me down?" I ask.

"As you wish." He says making me shiver again before setting me on my feet. He waits until I'm steady before stepping away, then flicks his eyes once in Jace's direction. "Until next time, Princess." He says before shadows swallow him and he disappears.

"Wait..." I cry out, but it's too late. He's already gone. Turning my gaze to Jace, I wait as he gets his temper under control.

"We're going home Ally." He declares, before striding away towards his own dorm room.

Letting myself into my dorm building, I try again to remember what happened and it all comes flooding back. The battle from the night before, the women from tonight and remembering my dream man showing up. The woman's voice asking me what I was, calling my dream man by his name and finally the dream I had of Jace and my parents.

Why had my father asked me to forgive him? What did they do to me? And how is Jace involved? More confused than ever, I focus on other details of the dream, like Jace's strange uniform and my parents pointed ears. "What am I?" I question out loud to the thankfully empty staircase. Grabbing my phone from my pocket I scroll down until I find Mrs Jones's number and hit dial.

"Alyssa?" She asks as soon as she answers, "what's wrong?" The concern in her voice makes me pause as I run up the last few steps and let myself into my shared flat. "Alyssa speak to me." She demands as I'm making sure no one's home.

"What am I?" I ask her.

I expect her to tell me I'm human but instead she sighs down the phone and utters two words before hanging up. "Come home."

Chapter Six

Lysais.

Everything spins around me as the darkness retreats, leaving me back in my own mind as he snarls and curses, "Fucking Half-breed." He shouts to the empty room, slamming his fist into the brick wall next to me as I try to force myself to remember what we'd just done. But this time it was blank. I knew I was missing time as we'd been in the camp before this room, and I had no memory of how we'd gotten here. "I fucking had her and he had to come along and ruin everything!"

"Ruin what?" I growl at him as his control slips with his rage, letting me vent my own anger at him.

"She remembered you, I thought that would break the damn magic," He fumed pacing the small room thinking. And all I could think was she remembered me and I'd bloody missed it! I could feel the despair of that thought nipping at my mind as I shut down any emotion tied to her.

"I should have taken his damn head, thinking he had the right to make us put her down." He shouts, drawing my attention back to this room as his temper flares again, and he launches a wooden chair into the wall.

"He's always had some balls on him," I taunt, smiling as I remember the time Jacin thought it would be a great idea to challenge me. He'd never made that same mistake again... until now obviously.

"Anger is a useless emotion," he suddenly sneers, reminding me of one of Father's many lessons on what he deemed 'pointless emotions'. I remembered the beatings that came with every word he spoke, as he literally hammered them home when I was six. It wasn't the first or the last of his lessons, but it was the first that he'd physically hit me. Flinching I dragged myself out of that particular memory, wondering when Balor been subjected to that lesson.

"I need her, but how?" he vents, not wanting me to answer. "Obviously her protector needs to be dealt with."

"Why do you even want to follow his orders?" I ask absolutely bewildered as to why anyone would choose to have anything to do with that monster.

"Because it should have been my life not yours." He explains distractedly.

"You can have my damn life, just leave her alone."

"Not without her I can't," he snarls at me, trying to make me flinch, but I was used to stronger monsters than him. "She's too important to him, I need to be the one to give her to him."

I can feel the dark magic taking hold of my mind again, and even though I know it's pointless to fight it I still try. "And with your help I'll succeed." He threatens before my world goes dark.

Chapter Seven

Alyssa.

Standing in the garden, staring at my parents, my jaw almost hits the floor. Lysias, the son of the Shadow King, stands beside them, staring at me from beneath his long dark lashes. Shadows twist and turn around him as he watches me. Holy Aine, he's handsome. My mind supplies, almost making me blush before I get control over myself again.

"Alysium? Are you even listening to me?" Mother's sweet voice breaks into my trace.

"He...he's going to train me." I stutter back, succinctly summing up what she's been explaining to me for the last twenty minutes. "But what about Jacin?" I ask, noticing that he's missing from our meeting.

"Jacin will still be your royal protector, but so will Lysias." I watch as her gaze flickers towards him and see the brief moment of fear shadow her purple eyes before it's gone.

"Why?" I question, whilst wondering what in the Fae I could need protecting from. I'm a princess, and I'm beloved by the citizens. What do I need protecting from, that it takes both Jacin and the Shadow prince? Just what are my parents keeping from me? I know there's something.

"Lysias is a fierce warrior just like Jacin, but he will be able to help train your magic, as well as your sword arm."

I gulp down my retort at that explanation, as I think about how my magic has begun to finally show itself, and how destructive it's been so far. Looking back at Lysias, I meet his ice-cold stare and feel a slight tug towards him. Forcing my feet to remain still, I look back at my parents and nod once.

"Good. We'll leave you to get acquainted then." She says, before picking up her flowered skirts and leaving us alone.

Looking at the ground, I try to still my racing heart before he hears it. "Princess?" His voice washes over me, making me shiver in delight *as his deep tone excites something inside me...*

I relive my most recent dream, trying to understand it, when my ringing phone makes me jump, just as the kettle clicks off. Jace's name blinks at me with a green speech bubble from WhatsApp. Remembering what happened last night, I feel my good mood from the dream evaporate. I'm beginning to think that my dreams aren't just dreams somehow. Swiping the answer bubble I wait for Jace to speak first.

"Ally?" He sounds too calm, he's been hiding things from me, so I refuse to answer. But he knows me, he knows I'm listening. "Be ready in half an hour." Is all he says before hanging up.

"Twat." I mutter at my phone, barely resisting the urge to throw it at the wall. Jace's betrayal hurts the most. I realised that before falling asleep last night. He's known all along that I wasn't crazy, yet no matter how confused I've been over the years, how crazy I thought I was—he never once told me it was all real!

Lilah I understand. She's been like a mother to me, but Jace was supposed to be my best friend. *How could he keep the truth from me?* Anger floods through me as I get out of bed and get ready to go home.

Half an hour later, I'm waiting outside my dorm building, looking up at it with a sense of foreboding. My gut is telling me that I won't be coming back again. Shivering, I remember Lysias from last night, as heat sweeps through me. Who is he to me? I wonder as I remember the way his voice slid down to my bones.

My smile dies when I see Jace walking slowly towards me with a bag slung over his shoulder. "Ready?" He asks. Gone is the joking friend I knew, and in his place is a calm, serious stranger. Nodding, I follow him towards the student parking and his sleek black car. Settling in the deep seat and fastening the belt with a loud click, I resigned myself to leaving. Glancing back once at the place I'd called home for the last two months, I say goodbye as Jace pulls out onto the road.

After ignoring Jace for almost an hour, I finally give in to the one question that's been burning my tongue. "Why?" I ask my voice barely above a whisper as hurt closes my throat.

"To protect you Ally, it was all to protect you." I can hear the pain in his voice as he admits that much to me. Frowning, I stare at the side of his face willing him to explain, but he says nothing more as he concentrates on the winding moor road.

We're nearly home, but all I feel is a deep wrongness inside, and I'm scared of what we're going to find. Taking deep breaths, I watch the empty moors flash by. Then the small town of Hutton-le-hole. Then, finally, we're driving down the small track that leads to the cottage.

As we draw near to where I've called home for the last three years, my sense of dread increases. Why is there smoke? Scared, I glance at Jace. I take in his fierce expression as he stares at the thin stream of black smoke coming from over the hill. I feel the car pick up speed as my gaze remains fixed on that smoke, watching as it gets bigger in the sky.. Then we're cresting the hill and a scream rips from my chest.

No! No! No! My mind shouts as I try to make sense of what I'm seeing. Our little cottage is pretty much burnt to the ground. As soon as the car stops I'm flinging open my door. "Lilah!" I scream at the burning, charred mess, willing her to answer me. I'm still running as I shout her name over and over. I'm about to throw myself into the flames when strong arms wrap around me from behind. Screaming until my throat burns, I fight Jace, kicking and scratching, but he refuses to let me go.

"Alyssa!" He calls over my screams, finally breaking through my terror. "She got out." His words register, and my screaming comes to an end. Looking back at him, I will him to explain how with my desperate eyes. "Look," he says, pointing off into the woods behind the cottage.

Narrowing my eyes, I try to see what he has, but come up blank, "what?" I ask confused.

"There in the ground," he says, pointing behind the cottage. Gouged into the grass and mud were two words; FIND ME.

"Where is she?" I ask him, not ready to believe that she really was ok.

"She'll have gone to a safe place."

"But this was a safe place."

"Not any more Ally," He stops to look into my eyes before continuing, "I don't think anywhere's safe now."

"What's going on Jace? Why is the cottage, our home, burnt down? How are the monsters real?" I ask each question tripping over the last, as I look to him for answers.

"I don't know Ally," he sounds as exasperated as I feel as I watch him closely, "you were meant to be safe here." I'm more confused by his answer.

"Jace. What are we?" I ask, dreading the answer but needing to know. He just looks at me frowning. "We're not human are we?" I press, already knowing we're not.

"No Ally, we are definitely not human." He says, watching me closely, "but I can't tell you what we are."

From my dreams, I had a sneaking suspicion that I knew what we were. I remember a musical voice, *What are you?* The huntress had asked last night, before she scented Lysias. Understanding dawns on me. She knows what we are, she has answers to my frantic questions. We need to find her again. "Jace, where has Lilah gone?" I hope he knows.

"I don't know Ally," He lets out a frustrated sigh, "we didn't plan for this."

"We—" My words break off as we both freeze, our attention turning to the woods behind the cottage.

Dark shapes take form amongst the trees. Each one looks like a person made of shadows. A shiver runs down my spine as I remember the other beings that attacked us in York, and my breath freezes in my lungs.

Glancing at Jace, *what the hell were we going to do?* I wonder as shadow after shadow comes to life. They make no sound, emerging from the forest like they didn't even exist. I pinch my arm hard, to convince myself that I'm awake and not hallucinating. *Nope it's real.*

"RUN!" Jace shouts, as I stumble backwards. "Get back to the car Ally."

Turning to go I look back once and see that Jace hasn't moved. I know I'm panicking but I can't seem to stop the rush of emotions, as I realise he's going to use himself to give me time to flee. *Like hell he is,* I think, searching the ground for anything I can use as a weapon.

There! Darting left, my hands grab a half burnt timber from the pile of rubble. Shaking, I walked back to Jace, prepared to fight beside him, even though I didn't know the first thing about combat. Shaking my head to rid the negative thoughts, I widen my legs—like they do in films—and swing my makeshift weapon to my shoulder.

Jace glances over at me once, shaking his head. "Don't you dare." I deadpan as he opens his mouth, "if you're staying, then so am I."

Sweat—partly from fear and partly from the warmth of the smouldering cottage—drips down my back as I turn back to face the shadow men. Steadying my arms, I wait until the first one crosses my invisible line and then swing for its head with all my strength. My burned piece of wood goes straight through the thing, throwing me off balance and making me spin, my feet tangling with each other. *Crap*, I think as I feel myself falling backwards. Everything slows down as I realise I've made a fatal error. I watch as the shadow man reaches out with clawed fingers, swiping for my chest as I fall. My eyes bounce to Jace, and I watch for a moment as he battles three shadow men with a sword.

Flashing images of a dark street in york and Jace standing wielding a sword, flash before my eyes briefly, before they're gone. *Where the fuck did he get a sword from?* I think momentarily confused.

Bracing myself to hit the ground, I let my eyes close. *I should have hit it by now, shouldn't I?* I think, before registering the warm hands gripping my upper arms a second later. My eyes fly open, staring straight into his.

Lysias! the hell is he doing here? I wonder briefly before he lifts me. He sets me on my feet for a second, before realising I don't know how to hit. With a grimace he shoves me behind his large back with one hand. The other I realise, smoothly draws a long sword that glows black. My mind fumbles to make sense of what's going, before he's moving, and I clamp my hands around his free hand holding myself to him.

Lysias moves as though I'm not hanging on to him as he spins, slashes and decapitates the shadow men with his strange sword, making his way efficiently back towards Jace. I begin to lose count of how many shadow men are hit by him. With a growl, he takes off two heads in one swipe, and then he's back to back with Jace with me sandwiched in the middle. Braced in a bubble of space between Jace and Ly, I watch as the shadow men waver in confusion, before they turn and flee back into the forest.

I can't breathe as the reality of what's just happened sinks in. We were attacked again by whatever those things were. My hands loosen from the death grip around Lysias' hand, and as I stumble, his whips back out to help steady me.

A snarl rips through the silence, dragging my attention away from my mini panic attack. Glancing around for another threat, I wonder where that noise came from. It could only belong to an animal, but there's just the three of us.

Jace steps toward me, his piece of wood raised as another snarl rips from his clenched mouth.

"Jace?" I question my voice wavering, as fear floods through me at the murderous expression on his face. Cringing back, I hit Lysias' hard chest and I realise I can't escape. Shaking my head rapidly, my breathing speeds up. I suddenly feel trapped as a pressure builds in my head. Pain splits my head in two as I scream, and a hard wave of air pushes away from me, hitting Jace solidly in his chest. His eyes widen in shock for a moment, before he's flying through the air. The pain stops for a second, and time seems to slow as I watch in horror. Jace hits the rubble that once was our home and time restarts. Suddenly my headache returns with a vengeance. Grabbing my head I scream.

Crouching, folding in on myself, I grip my head tighter, as

if I can stop the pain if only I hold on harder. What the hell is happening to me? I wonder as I see Jace flying backwards through the air.

"Alyssa?" Jace's frantic voice draws my attention as the pain begins to fade, "are you ok?" I know I need to answer, but *what am I supposed to say? No, I'm crazy and dangerous?* I feel his warm hands on mine as he tries to draw them away from my head, but I'm scared that if I let go the pain will come back.

"She'll be ok," a deep voice answers him, making me shiver and finally open my eyes. Jace is bending over me, his eyes searching mine, while Lysias stares at me from a distance, his gaze evaluating me where I crouch. His eyes are bitterly cold as he watches me.

"What the hell was that?" I question them both.

"Nothing..." Jace says as Lysias says, "Magic, Princess."

Glancing between the two of them, my mouth opens, then closes as I flounder for some response. Removing my hands I point at Lysias, "who...no what are you?" I question not knowing if I really want to know the answer.

"He's leaving," Jace spits out, before Lysias can answer me. Confused, I glance back at him. *Why does he hate him?*

"Jace what the hell is going on?" I demand, "and no more lies." I hiss before he tells me again that he doesn't know.

"I'm not allowed to tell you," he whispers, staring into my eyes, willing me to understand.

"Then you," I demand, my eyes focusing on Lysias, where he stands looking like this whole ordeal bores him, "what the hell is going on?"

Lysias opens his mouth as if he's going to answer my question, but scoffs instead, before turning his back on us and walking away.

Nobhead, I think as my mouth opens, "Oi!" I scream at his back as my anger flares to life, "who the hell do you think you are, ignoring me and walking away."

"A prince," he mocks, before turning fully to face me with a cruel smile "I'll be seeing you Princess," he adds laughing cruelly before disappearing in a vortex of shadows.

Looking back at Jace, I arch an eyebrow, "why can't you tell me what's going on Jace?" I ask, trying to calm my anger and failing.

I watch as he drops his gaze to the ground, struggling with some internal battle before he sighs and sits before me, "all I can tell you is that you're special, and as soon as I can tell you everything I will." He pauses before continuing. "Can you accept that?" he asks quietly.

Mulling over his cryptic answer, I groan as I try to put the puzzle together without all the pieces. "What happens if I can't?" I question quietly.

He shrugs at me before meeting my gaze, his brown eyes are filled with tears. "I'd tell you everything if I could, Ally you've got to believe that I would, but I think it would kill you if I did." He explains as tears slip down his cheeks, "it would be so much easier if I could, I hate this." He stops on a sob and scrubs at his tears.

Softening, I lean towards him. "Just tell me one thing?" I ask, watching hope surface in his eyes as he nods, "are my dreams real?" I wait, scared to even breathe as the hope fades from his eyes and I know the answer before he opens his mouth.

"Yes, they're real." He says quietly.

It's like a slap to the face, making me flinch away from him, shaking my head as my heart breaks. This whole time he's known I wasn't crazy, he's watched me struggle and done nothing but convince me to take those damn pills. How could he? How did my best friend betray me like that? I wonder, backing further away from him. "Why?" I whisper, knowing there's nothing he can say that will make this right, nothing.

"To protect you, everything has been to protect you." He answers brokenly.

"And Lilah?" I ask.

Jace just nods, confirming that they both knew I wasn't crazy but kept up the pretence for so long. All I can do is stare at him as my world crashes down around me. Remembering my dreams I look at them in a new light. *The balls, the dresses, the creatures.*

They're all real. So, what am I?

A freak, my mind supplies sarcastically. Snorting quietly, I pick myself up and focus on what I need to do, because if I only focus on his betrayal I know I'll fall apart. "So what do we do now?"

"Honestly?" He asks, not really needing me to answer, "I don't know. Lilah knew what to do, not me, and she's..." He shrugs and trails off as we both look over the ruined cottage.

My heart sinks as I look at the destruction, remembering the once pristine cottage and how Lilah would always be bustling about doing something, muttering to herself. "Where would she have gone Jace, you must know."

When he doesn't immediately answer, I glance across at him, watching as he racks his brain for any answer to give me. As he finally looks up, I realise just how screwed we are, "I don't Ally. We never planned to be separated, only to wait here until..."

Pain spears through my head briefly, making me scream and cutting off whatever he was about to say. It fades as soon as he stops talking, meeting his worried gaze. I understand why he can't tell me everything.

"What have you remembered so far?" he asks, serious as he watches me. It's like looking at a complete stranger. Gone is the carefree jokester I know replaced, by someone focused and serious. A warrior.

"Just bits and pieces," I sigh frustrated before continuing, "balls and dresses mainly, they changed recently though. You were in one but you looked different Jace," I explain pausing to see his expression, "you had pointy ears and your skin was lighter..." my voice dies off as I realise how ridiculous I sound.

"What else Ally, obviously you remember the shadow man, you've always remembered him."

"Lysias." I cut him off, "but even he's different." I mumble as Jace's expression changes, darkens at my words. "In my memories he's lighter somehow, his eyes are warmer...I don't know I can't explain it, just that he seems different here and where-ever that was."

"Hmmmm," is all Jace says before turning to search the rubble.

"Jace...in York I met some people," I pause as his head snaps towards me.

"What people?" He questions.

"Two women, although I don't know if one of them could be called a woman, she definitely wasn't human, but she was a woman I suppose—"

"Ally stop," Jace commands, cutting off my babble, "focus. When did you meet them?"

"Last night, before Lysias took me home. She knew Jace," I look at him as hope flares to life inside me, "she knew what I was."

"Do you know who she was?" Jace asks cautiously, in case he triggers something I'm not ready for.

"No, but the man and Lysias called her a Huntress." Jace's frown deepens at my words. He knows what she was.

"And the other woman?"

I shrug because she didn't really speak much, "I think she was human, like..." I trail off realising we're not human, so she wasn't really like us. His eyes soften as he realises what I just figured out, "she used magic I think."

I can see the cogs working inside his mind as he tries to come up with some sort of plan. After a while he focuses on me, determination shining through him, "we're going back to York." He states before waltzing off to his car.

Chapter Eight

Lysais.

We'd almost arrived too late. One of the Demoran guarding that hovel which they'd called home, had come to inform us that two people had turned up at the ruins and we'd traveled the shadows to arrive just as my minions began their attack. I'd ordered them to attack anyone who came sniffing around, annoyed that the Fae residing in the place had managed to escape me. She was the key I needed to unlock Alyssa's secrets and break the binds on her power.

I'd listened to Alyssa's conversation the night before, and heard her question what she was, before shadow walking to Jacin's accommodation just as his phone had rung. The same female voice who'd been talking to Alyssa spoke again. It hadn't taken much prompting for his subconscious to conjure up the images I'd needed to find this 'cottage' and the mystery woman. Lilah.

It was pitch black as my Demoran and I had surrounded the small cottage, closing in silently on the woman humming inside. I don't know what tipped her off that she wasn't alone, but her humming suddenly stopped as she whirled towards the front door. "Come in, Shadow Lord." She'd demanded in a stern voice, moments before I pushed open the front door, staring murder at the short woman as she surprised me. Of course I was wearing his face but I was surprised she recognised him. "You can not have her." She stated, before walking from the room, confirming that we had found the missing princess.

"Why not?" I asked, coldly stalking her through the small front room, not in any hurry knowing she'd be trapped in there. "They really do make this easy," I muttered the moment before I stepped into the empty bedroom.

Where had she fucking gone? I fumed, tossing the whole bed against the wall thinking she might be hiding underneath it, before pacing the room trying to see what I'd missed and sure enough there it was. The subtle scent of Brownie magic. *She was a bloody Brownie!* Rage threatened to devour me as I realised I'd underestimated the small woman, believing she was light Fae, not a sniveling Brownie.

A blade of shadows formed in my left hand as I ran at the nearest wall. I destroyed it with a blast of magic in my desperation to get outside and reach her before she escaped. Pausing, I let my senses take over as I hunted her. There. Her scent was to the right. Smiling, I turned her way, following her to the edge of the trees. But she'd already fled, leaving only a destroyed bush and the scent of witch magic hanging in the air. Rage consumed me as I ordered my Demoran to destroy the cottage.

Dragging myself back to the present, I'm cursing myself from the shadows. I hadn't been specific enough in my instructions to the Demoran and she'd almost been hurt—if it hadn't been for Him forcing us to move faster she might have been.

We'd arrived as Jacin told her to run, but Alyssa was too pure for own good. I'd been shocked when she'd picked up that piece of wood and stood her ground instead of running.

She'd looked fierce, like the warrior she was at heart beneath this frail human glamour. I see what drew you to her Brother, I internally comment, riling him up just for fun, as we continue watching in secret before one of the Demoran had targeted her as a threat and lunged for her, forcing me to intervene.

I could still feel the heat of her skin as we'd pressed her close to us, effortlessly battling the Demoran as their confusion immobilised them. Stupid creatures really, only able to follow orders and not think for themselves anymore. He'd liked having her close again, I could still feel his hunger for Alyssa as if it was my own. It made me sick, feeling how He felt for her. I'd never love anyone, love made you fear, which made you weak. *Just look at you Brother, trapped as you are because you fell in love with her.*

The sound of their bickering drew me back to the present as I listened happily to her shouting at Jacin. He'd lied to her, the stupid boy and sown the seeds I needed to drag them apart. I could see the mistrust shining in her eyes as she demanded the truth and he with-held it. I could and would use that against them.

Chapter Nine

Alyssa.

"Again." Lysias demands, as my arse hits the floor for the hundredth time this afternoon. Sweat sticks any loose hair to my face and neck, before dripping down my face. Glancing down I dismiss the mud splatters on my grey training leathers, as he stands glaring down at me again. Shaking my head and pushing myself up from the ground, I get back to my feet, planting them firmly apart as I wait for him to come at me again.

"Why do I even need to know this?" I question, wondering what the point of learning hand-to-hand combat is. "I have magic, why could I possibly need to learn this stuff?" I pout at him.

"What if you can't use your magic?" He says with more patience than I deserve, "What if your opponent is resistant to your magic?"

"Fine," I agree with his reasoning, even if I don't think I'll ever have to use my hands in a fight. He's on me before I'm ready, using his shadows against me as his clenched fist flashes towards my face. Without thinking I grab his wrist and use his momentum against him.

Spinning, I'm ready to block the kick aimed at my stomach with crossed wrists. Shoving him back, I breathe deeply as I watch to see where his next attack will come from. Smiling deviously Lysias disappears, swallowed by shadows. Spinning slowly my eyes bounce around, never settling on one thing for long, trying to find where he'll reappear.

I hesitate when my instincts scream at me to look up. Snapping my head back on my neck I watch, eyes wide as he appears mid-air and drops down, forcing me to the floor yet again. My chest heaves against his thighs with each breath as he straddles me, his blue eyes only inches from my own. My blood races as I stare, overly aware of our bodies touching. Smiling, I run my eyes over his form fitted leathers, appreciating the way they're moulded to his perfect body.

"Like what you see Princess?" He whispers arrogantly, knowing the *effect he has on me.*

"You wish," I spit before using my magic and forcing him off of me as I roll on top of him. I realise my mistake too late, when I feel myself settle above his hips and rub against something hard. Gasping, my eyes flash to his, where hunger and lust burns for a second before he flips us again.

Water from the grass seeps through my hair but I don't care as I watch his lips lower toward mine, before closing them and waiting.

His tortured groan is the only indication I get before his weight disappears completely and I know he's run again. Letting out a loud groan, I wonder what the Aine I'm even doing. His father is waging war on my own family, me and him could never happen.

Gasping, my eyes fly open focusing on the familiar walls of my dorm room, as my chest heaves. We've been back in York for a week now, searching for those two women, with no luck. I'm still registered on my course but I've not been attending any of my lessons. *What's the point? It's not like we'll be sticking around. I think sadly.*

Rolling over, my dream repeats in my mind. Obviously I'd been trained to fight at some point, but for what? Even my dream-self didn't know. I need training, I decide wondering if Jace could help me. I'd seen him fight at the cottage so he definitely knows how, maybe it would trigger more of my memories. And even if it doesn't I can't go on like this, I won't be a liability.

Those shadow men—I still don't even have a name for them I realise-aren't going to stop, so I have to be ready for when they show up next. *I'm not some ruddy damsel in distress*, I remind myself angrily as I grab my phone to message Jace. Pressing the lock button my eyes widened at the time, 4.05, "bloody hell it's too early," I muttered to myself before unlocking it and pulling up Jace's contact.

I need training. I fire off in our WhatsApp chat before dropping my phone on the quilt next to me as I flop back down. Not expecting him to answer at this time of day, I almost screech as it chimes, scaring the crap out of me.

I agree, meet me outside in 20 mins. He responds, making my eyes roll at his command. I don't bother texting back before searching my drawers for the workout gear I've not had a chance to wear yet.

Fifteen minutes later, I'm dressed in loose sweatpants and a tight vest-top, with a sports bra securing my moderate breasts in place as I lean against the cold stone of my dorm, shivering in the early morning chill. Jace is dressed similarly, with a frown pulling at his brows as he rounds the corner and walks towards me.

"You ready for this Ally?" He asks seriously, appraising my outfit quickly, before meeting my eyes again. I nod once before he immediately turns, and starts jogging towards the main campus building, "come on then." He shouts over his shoulder when I don't automatically follow. Stifling a curse as I realise we're going running-I hate running-I sprint to catch up.

My face resembles a tomato as I stumble through the gates into Museum Gardens, two hours later, feeling like I'm about to die. Sucking in air as if it's about to run out, I realise how out of shape I've become since leaving the cottage. After jogging around what must have been the whole of York I'm bent in two, panting while Jace swings his arms leisurely.

"Ok, now your training starts," he says, drawing my attention from the slowly lightning sky as I stretch out my back, and grinning at the groan that slips loose.

Bloody sadist, I think spitefully as my lungs burn and the stitch in my side throbs again. Worst idea ever Alyssa, I scold myself silently, as I wait for whatever comes next. Sucking in a deep breath I glance around, noticing we're alone for now, even with the sky lightning from pink to light blue.

The November air has me shivering as it chills the sweat on my skin, distracting me from everything as it rattles the last few leaves clinging to trees and bushes. Movement to my left, makes my eyes widen as Jace takes a slightly menacing step towards me. "We'll start off easy, Ally," he explains slowly and I nod, waiting uneasily as he stops within touching distance. "Do you remember any of your training from…before?"

"A little," I answer in a small voice, as I thought back to my dream last night. With Lysais' voice in my head, I move my legs until I have them shoulder width apart. Once I feel that my feet are planted firmly, I nod letting him know I'm ready. Watching him closely I try to see what he's thinking, but his expression gives nothing away. I scream as he suddenly charges for me.

I'm still screaming as his arms wrap around my middle, lifting me off the ground and then I'm sailing through air as the dickhead tosses me aside. Growling, I roll as I hit the ground, rising slightly into a crouch. I watch his feet pounding towards me. Staying close to the ground, I wait trying to grab his ankle and pull him off balance, but he jumps as I lurch forward and my hand grabs nothing but air.

The air whistles, giving me just enough time to jerk backwards as his foot narrowly misses my face, knocking me off balance as my arse hits the cold ground. Jace doesn't give me any time to catch my breath or move as his fist aims straight for my face and I panic.

That strange pressure builds inside me, and I grab for it instinctively before forcing it towards Jace. His fist is inches away from my face when a blast of air knocks him, forcing him a foot backwards. A laugh bubbles out of me at the shock on his face, moments before what I did hits me. I made air do what I wanted. No, I couldn't have done that. Could I? I marvel before standing and walking over to him. "Jace what's happening to me, what the hell did I just do?" I ask uncertainty, reaching down to help him up.

"It's…" Jace pauses as he looks me over, clearly torn about how to explain this.

"Magic?" I ask in disbelief.

"Yes it is, youngling." A woman's voice rings out behind me, making me jump before I spin around, and pinned her with what I hoped was a death glare before she continues, "and there's more where that comes from Honey."

Confused, I just stare at whoever she is, taking in her tight black leathers and twin swords poking over her shoulders, before my voice finally snaps out, "and who the hell are you?" I ask sharply, my patience clearly at its end.

"Matilda," she answers easily, tilting her head to the side like a bird watching its prey, "and who are you?" She asks back, circling us both. "Which one maybe?" She states when neither of us gives her an answer.

Turning to keep her in my sight, trying to figure out what she is, as she watches us like a bug under a magnifying glass, I know she's doing the same with us. She draws in a deep breath through her nose, reminding me of someone else, but I can't place who as she moves again. Watching her carefully, I notice the feline way she moves, her feet light on the ground almost like she's dancing instead of walking.

"No, not witch, their magic smells different" Matilda states as she sniffs the air again, "you're something much older and rarer." She muses, tapping her chin as she thinks.

"I don't know what I am." I tell her honestly, my eyes flicking to Jace and back to her green ones.

"But he does, doesn't he,"

"Yes."

"Well?" Matilda asks, narrowing her eyes at Jace, who refuses to answer, "fine keep your secrets, but you can't be letting off magic like that and think no one will notice."

"Probably," I answer when Jace remains mute, "it's not like I can control it." I mumble letting my frustration bleed into my voice.

"Ah, you'll need a Coven then."

"A what?"

"A Coven," Matilda deadpans as if I should know what the heck she's going on about, "God you really know nothing," she states before flashing forward. One minute she's five steps away and the next she has my wrist in her hand, her nail pricking my skin. A drop of blood wells to the surface and before I can stop her, she licks it.

Disgust floods through me as her eyes close in pleasure for a moment. She tastes my blood, letting out a breathy sigh before stepping away almost as fast as she approached. Shocked, all I can do is stare as my mind tries to tell me what she is, but I don't want to believe it.

Vampire. Shaking my head, I look from her to Jace, trying to tell him with my eyes what I'm thinking. Jace, who can't meet my eyes. And I realise he's known all along what she is. Her hiss has my head snapping back to her, as she recoils another step, "Ancients." She spits at us, making me even more confused, "you shouldn't be here." I blink and Jace is standing between us protecting me from her.

"Says Who?" I ask, peeking around Jace's hulking body, willing her to say more.

"Say your own kind," she spits back, retreating another step as if we were contagious or something.

"Well, here we are. So deal with it." I snap back, sick not just of her superior attitude, but with everything my life has become. There are so many gaps in my memory, but I can't even push for more information or my brain explodes. Shuddering I remember the pain from last week.. Let's just say I'm not looking to relive the experience any time soon.

"You are, but you need to go back as soon as possible." Matilda mutters almost as if she's speaking to herself rather than us as she paces the gardens, "I'm surprised you've lasted this long without drawing attention."

"Great, go back where?" I ask, interrupting her mutterings.

"To your own world," her tone is clipped, like she's speaking to a crazy person who should know what she's on about.

"And that would be?" I sass back at her, gaining a warning look from Jace and I know I'm walking a fine line but nothing she's said so far has made my head hurt.

"The land of the F..." Pain blocks out whatever she's saying, as I squeeze my eyes shut and grip my head. I refuse to make a sound this time as the pain spears through my mind for a few minutes before the world returns.

"What the hell is wrong with her?" Matilda's voice registers as the pain dims.

"There's a block on her mind, a powerful one that causes her pain when she hears certain information regarding her past." Jace's rational tone has me opening my eyes again, staring at the back of his legs. Confused, I follow them up to his worried expression and realise I'm crouched down. "You ok Ally?" He asks, worry turning his voice into a low growl, before shifting his attention back to Matilda.

"I'm good," I tell him, watching as his shoulders relax, and standing back up as a more normal headache starts up.

"Ah, things make a little more sense now," Matilda says, drawing my focus back to her. Imitating her stance, my hip pops out and my head tilts the same direction as hers as she regards us both with a frown. "You're coming with me then," she states flatly, nodding to herself as she makes the decision.

"Coming where?" Jace snarls threateningly, before going ramrod straight.

"To London, I can't just leave you here wandering around can I?" Matilda explains rolling her eyes as though we're stupid.

"Why not, we've already been here for years," I tell her.

"Well you weren't releasing powerful magic then were you." She fires back sarcastically.

"I guess not." I agree reluctantly.

"Great, it's settled then, I'll meet you in front of the Minister at dusk, you do know where that is right?" She asks, waiting for one of us to nod before she disappears.

"Damn Vampires," Jace snarls viciously at the empty spot where she was standing, as if he'd just woken back up. "We're not going with the likes of her." He snaps, turning to glare at me.

"It's not like we have many other options is it?" I point out shrugging.

"Suppose not," he agrees begrudgingly, after a couple of minutes silence.

"Guess this means no more training today?"

Jace shakes his head at me, before walking back towards the entrance, "Wanna race back?" He asks, throwing me a smile over his shoulder as he falls back into the funny best friend I've always known, "last one back buys lunch." He gambles.

"You're on," I laugh back at him before running through the entrance and gaining a tiny head start. I'm still laughing as I round another corner and see my uni dorm building across the small car park. Glancing over my shoulder I laugh louder, I'm going to bloody win, I congratulate myself, seeing him a few steps behind me. Until I notice his cocky grin, confusing me for a moment before he picks up his pace and draws level for a second before overtaking me.

"Damn it," I groan as I watch his back, forcing myself to run faster, but I can't seem to catch him as my grin slips from my face.

"You got way too cocky way too fast," he grins at me when I finally stop in front of my dorm, trying to catch my breath, "it's all about pacing yourself Ally." He tells me sounding superior as he watches me bend over, clutching my side as a stitch burns.

"Fuck off, like you know anything about pacing yourself," I gasp at him with a smile, "lunch is on me then." I mumble mentally assessing how much money I have left in my account.

"Definitely," his grin is so big it almost takes over his face.

"Do you think we'll ever come back here?" I ask wistfully, looking over the uni buildings I'd only just gotten to know.

"Probably not," he answers sadly but seriously.

"Oh well, it was good while it lasted," I can't keep the disappointment from my voice as I turn back to him.

"Yeah it was, but it's like when we were younger Ally, when we moved around before finding the cottage." He tries to smile and lift my spirits, but all I can think about is the mess our lives have become.

"I suppose so, I hated leaving then too," I answered back, stealing my heart against the pain of leaving again. "We still need to find Lilah." I mumble, glancing at his face and shrinking from the pain I see in his eyes.

"We'll find her Ally," Jace said using his stern, no nonsense tone that makes me want to believe him. Nodding once, I let myself inside and slowly made my way to my room.

Chapter Ten

Balor.

Watching from the shadows, I almost growl as Jacin and Alyssa cross into the deserted park, what a weakling I snarl contemptuously in my head as she doubles over. It's like watching a newborn lamb as she gulps down air. What are you up to? I wonder, a moment before there's a tug inside my mind, as He pulls against my hold. Strengthening the dark tendrils that keep him contained, I return my attention back to Alyssa, watching her plant her feet steadily on the hard ground, giving me my answer.

Intrigued, I watched their fight a moment longer as her muscle memory comes alive, and I can't look away as she quickly regains some of the hand to hand combat skills I'd seen in His memories. They hadn't used weapons but I'm sure that would probably be the same, given half the chance. Her magic bothered me, it still seemed to be out of her grasp.

But it was seeping out slowly, I noticed as a sudden ripple of light danced over her skin, and I smelt the tantalising scent of her earth magic wanting to come out and play. However, those binds of hers remained strong enough to keep the majority of it locked down and flood her mind with imagined pain if triggered. It was impressive magic to keep a powerful creature, such as her, bound. The only problem was she was attracting attention.

More and more creatures were flocking to York since she'd come back from that shack they'd called home, as though the dam was slowly fracturing. They didn't know who or what they were searching for, but I was certain Alyssa was unconsciously calling them here. A rustle to my right yanked my head to the side, meeting a pair of yellow eyes staring right at me through my shadows.

Moving like a ghost I approached slowly, not wanting to spook it. We'd managed to grab some of the nastier ones but, like this one, there would be others we'd missed. Inching closer to bushes, I let my shadows rush out snaring whatever the hell those eyes belonged to in an iron grip. Glancing back once at Alyssa, I watched her block a kick from Jacin, before forcing the creature before me to the camp I'd established on the outskirts of York.

Over the last week we'd forced all the feral dark creatures, who followed the pull towards the city, into this one field. They'd been calling this world home undetected for over a millenia after the gates were closed. Abandoned in the human world, having to hide and fade into these disgustingly weak creature's myths and legends. Such a shame. I'd been surprised that they'd left the dark recesses of their caves, to hunt the magic they could barely remember.

It didn't matter that we were on the opposite side of the city, when the shock-wave of powerful magic washed over the camp. Our skin tingled, the bond in our chest rattled, squeezing the breath from our lungs as I tried suppressing it again. Only one person's power would cause such a powerful reaction in us and, from the leering look on Drafnoughl's face, it wasn't just the bond that made us feel her magic this far away.

"Whhaatt waas thhaat?" He asked in the drawn out way of the forest Fae that had been abandoned here, after the big cleansing of this world.

"Nothing that concerns you." I snapped drawing his attention back as his tongue flicked out to wet his lips, like he was tasting Alyssa in the air.

"Hhhmmmmm, ddeeliciiousss," he mumbled with a shiver, as another shock-wave of her power rushed over the camp, making more of the Fae here scent the air. Our gaze looked out over the Fae assembled here, noting each race of creature as they tipped their head to the sky.

Their new queen had been hiding here for years, and now her magic was calling them to her. Some that had been abandoned here were ancient Fae that no longer graced our home worlds.

Banshees, Forest nymphs, Dryads and Bokhams had all flocked to York each night. And, if she got near the coast, the sea Fae hiding there would also answer the siren call she was emitting. She was lucky we'd intercepted the Fae in this camp, and clamped them in bargains that kept them far away from her, but with this amount of power flooding out of her she wouldn't—couldn't—remain hidden in this city for long.

She'd already gained the attention of a Huntress, who would find her next? I wondered with a snarl, as I barked out orders for the Fae here to move out of the city and into the countryside, before turning to the shadows and speeding to where my tracking spell led. We didn't see what triggered Alyssa but her magic had flared bright. So I had not been surprised to find the Vampiress, already in the gardens with her.

"Fuck!" I snarled from the shadows as we overheard the end of their conversation, they were going to London, to the vampire coven. We'd learned all we could about the hierarchy of the creatures left here after the sealing, but most—like the Fae—the humans had relegated to being myths and legends. Scary stories that adults told their children. But the London coven was the hub in charge of everything. Being one of the oldest vampire lairs in the world meant it set the rules and nobody broke them.

If she got the protection of the London coven she'd be even harder to steal away. I needed to sort that out, and fast. We couldn't lose the small amount of control we had over the situation, but who could I turn to our way of thinking?

Staring at Alyssa across the park I realised two things one; Lysais hadn't been stupid in his choice of mate, she was powerful and intoxicating and two; her power was going to be a bitch to control when it was all let loose after we broke her bindings. And when that happened she'd be magnificent...we just needed her to be ours when that happened.

Chapter Eleven

Alyssa.

"Alysium?" Jacin's voice sings from somewhere behind me, where I crouch behind the biggest fountain I could find in the garden. Not wanting company, I consider running away like I did from our tutors earlier. Absolute garbage, that's what they were trying to fill my head with. Shaking my head, I refuse to remember what they'd been trying to tell me. Furious, I've been sitting here for the last few hours, just staring at the flower bed in front of me. "I know you're out here." He tells me as he's followed the protectors bond to find me in the first place.

Urggg! I scream inside my head before waving my hand in the air so he can see it over the lip of the fountain. I hear his laugh before I actually see him, as I bring my knees to my chest. "What?" I snap at him, letting him know just how bad my mood is.

"I came to check on you, how you doing?" He asks even knowing I'm not in the mood.

"Fine." I snap out, before letting my head drop to rest on my knees, "just peachy." I can't help the sarcasm that laces my words and right now I don't care either.

"Come on Ally, this isn't you?" He patiently tells me as if he knows me better than I know myself. I guess sometimes it's true, but not always.

"I just..." I begin, breaking off when I can't even put into words what's made me so angry, "not everyone's the same Jacin, why can't they see that?" I finally finished, raising my head to look at him.

"The wars have been going on too long Ally..."

"I know that, it's been waging since before I was born," I interrupt, "but that's no excuse for what they did in there." I hiss, waving back towards the palace.

"It's hurt everyone in some way, and no, that doesn't excuse what they did. But you need to understand that The King of Shadow's is responsible for the pain they've felt when a loved one hasn't returned."

Frustrated I sigh, trying to let go of my anger, Jacin's sense of calm reaching me through the guardian bond as he sits down next to me. "When did you get so smart?" I ask, trying to lighten my mood.

"About the same time that you got so crazy," he jokes but I can't smile. Since I came into my magic, my moods have been unstable. Flying into a rage at the littlest thing that I don't agree with, or breaking down at anything that's remotely sad.

"Haha," I mumble back, knocking his shoulder with mine, "where's Lysias anyway?" I ask.

"Pacing in another garden," he shrugs, as he lets me know I'm not the only one affected by what our stupid tutors said.

Pushing out a breath, I force my anger deep down inside before I begin setting the flowers on fire. "Which one Jacin?" I ask slightly calmer than before.

"Statue garden," Jacin pauses as I stand, clearly warring with whatever he wants to say to me.

"Just spit it out, Jacin." I tell him, having no patience to not be direct.

"Just be careful with him Ally." His voice is the most serious I've ever heard it, as he looks up at me. I feel his worry down our bond before I shut it down, and nod letting him know I heard him before striding away.

I know he'll follow me, he has to, but at least he does it from a distance when I need him to. Unlike others that guard me. Leaving the garden, I put my court mask firmly back in place and soften my pace so my dress skirt barely moves, as I make my way to the one garden in this place that no one ever goes.

The walk is thankfully short, so it's not long until I'm slipping past the steel gates and away from the prying eyes of court life. Releasing a breath I didn't even realise I'd been holding, I start searching. Each statue in here was gifted, at one time or another, by the royal family of the Shadow Realm. There was another filled with other fantastical beasts, but this one was different. I've been fascinated by them since I was younger, making up stories behind each one. Of course He'd be here, I think, smiling to myself as I pass a statue of a horse looking creature, then one of a man with fangs delicately carved into his gaping mouth.

Nearing the back of the garden I find him pacing, just as Jacin said he was, beneath a statue that's always creeped me out. Looming above Lysias is an exact liking of his father, when he was around Lysias' age now. Looking from that to his son, the resemblance is striking; they could be twins.

"Hey," I speak softly as he paces like a cornered animal, instead of the Shadow Prince that he is. Black eyes flash to meet mine as my voice breaks the silence, making my steps pause for a moment.

"Princess," he snarls at me, making my heart race.

Bang! My eyes fly open at the sound. I glance around my now empty room, disorientated before I realise I'd fallen asleep. Packing up my small dorm had taken less time than I thought it would, as did phoning the admin office to let them know I wouldn't be continuing with my studies.

Bang, bang, bang! The knocking starts up again, even as I try drowning it out under the pillow now smushed over my face, but whoever it is persists. I groan as I drag myself off my bed to the front door. Resting my forehead against the cold wood door, I look through the small peephole at a bending but empty hallway. Frowning I open the door slowly, sticking my head out and searching every inch of the deserted hall. "Stupid students" I mutter frustrated at the obvious prank. I'm going to close the door when my eyes fall upon an envelope with my name on it.

Curious, I snatch the letter up and slam the door behind me, walking to the front room before opening it.

Dear Princess,

I know you don't understand everything, but in time you will and you'll come to understand that I'm not the good guy in your story. I cannot say too much, but please be wary around me in future. My time is short but I need you to know that your friend from the cottage is safe, she is hiding out with powerful friends.

Don't try to find me as I'm sure that I will find you again when the time is right, all I ask is for your forgiveness.

Yours Always.

The letter's short, just a couple of lines, but I know it's from Lysias…he's the only one that calls me princess. Frustrated, I feel my anger rising, as I reread it finding no real answers to any of my questions. It just leaves me with more, how does he know about Lilah? And what does he mean he's not the good guy?

Urgg! I groan, screwing up the small sheet of cream coloured paper in my hands, ready to throw it across the room, before rethinking and stuffing it in the back pocket of my jeans. Shaking my head, I walk back to my room slowly and stand in the doorway looking over the few boxes of stuff. Taking a deep breath I grab one and begin the arduous task of taking them all downstairs, ready to go in Jace's car.

Half an hour later, I'm sitting on the doorstep of my dorm waiting for Jace to arrive, as the sun is beginning to set, painting the sky pink. Closing my eyes, I wonder what the future holds for us. Letting out a sigh, I open my eyes and watch students as they mill about going to and from uni, wishing I was just like them instead of whatever the hell I actually am.

"What you thinking about?" Jace's voice brings me out of my mind as he saunters towards me.

"Nothing much," I reply, shrugging as he reaches me.

"You ready?" He asks, watching me closely as I nod and push myself to my feet. Unlocking the door, I wedge it open with a box before grabbing another and walking towards the small car park near the dorm. Back and forth we walk, until he places the last box in his big boot before slamming it shut. "Come on short stuff," he smiles at me, trying to make this easier on me, "let's go hand our keys in and get out of here."

Sighing again, I try to let go of the sadness, and follow him to student services, ignoring the hollow feeling that's growing inside me as my world continues to fall apart. It doesn't take long to hand our dorms back over to the kind lady behind the desk. She has us sign some forms, and asks us again if there's anything she can do to make us stay as we shake our heads.

I watch in silence as we drive out of campus, and Jace grips my leg once before turning onto Gillygate as I say my silent goodbyes to uni life. "What are our lives going to be like now?" I ask him, turning in my seat.

"I don't know Ally" he answers honestly, glancing at me briefly before returning his attention to the busy road, as we inch our way towards the minister. "Maybe we'll go home." He mutters wistfully as I return my gaze to the street outside our car.

"Maybe," I mumble, not really knowing where home is any more.

Matilda's waiting for us in the taxi drop off area as we pull up, "you both ready to go?" She asks climbing in the back.

"Do we really have a choice?" I ask sarcastically as I look at her over my shoulder.

"Not really," she agrees, looking a little apologetic as she meets my eyes.

"So where are we going?" I ask, trying to figure out where my life would take me next.

"London," she states looking out the window instead of at me.

"Great, that's super helpful" I mumble sarcastically, before looking forward as we pass over Lendal Bridge on our way out of York.

"Hampstead Gardens, to be precise, I need to speak with my Coven." Matilda mentioned vaguely, before dropping a thick black pair of sunglasses over her eyes. Shutting us out as we continued driving.

One glance at Jace let me know that her attitude pissed him off as well, as I put the destination in the sat-nav.

Music echoes through the halls, as I drag my feet, shuffling slowly towards the ballroom. Mother explained to me earlier that my attendance is not optional at tonight's celebrations, but she didn't say I had to be on time either. Grinning, I picture her annoyance at my lack of respect for punctuality, almost letting out a snort of laughter.

I'm livid at her for making me attend another damn ball. She knows how much I hate these damn things. But —as she also likes to remind me constantly—one day I'll be Queen and have to hold these damn things regularly.

Not for years to come, my mind supplies in reassurance, my mood souring further as I get closer to the ballroom. I don't even know what we're meant to be celebrating tonight, I'm sure it's something dull and outdated.

"Alysium," Ari's voice sings down the corridor as she hurries towards me, "hurry up your Mother's asking where you are." Ah Arielle, my faithful friend, always trying to keep me on time. Smiling, I make my steps slower just to annoy her a little. Frustrated, she throws her hands in the air before gesturing in my direction, a blast of wind almost knocking me off my feet as she uses her magic to force me to hurry.

"Not fair Ari," I complain as I get closer, and her smile widens at my discomfort. She's a few months older than me so her magic manifested already, while mine is still nowhere in sight.

"Well next time you might not flout your good mother's patience," she states, before sticking her tongue out at me and sweeping me into the ballroom.

"Princess Alysium Beltymne of Agenia." The master of ceremonies announces somberly to the gathered members of my mother's court, making everyone stop and stare as I enter. My cheeks blaze pink, making my embarrassment clear to everyone. He opens his mouth to speak further, quickly shutting it at my death glare.

Refraining from shaking my head, I try descending the stairs gracefully—failing spectacularly as I stumble over my dress—searching for Mother among the mass of creatures. Submerging myself in the crowd, I watch Pixies flutter by leaving glowing trails behind them. Scantily clad water Nymphs gyrate fluidly against other dancers. My head whips round at the low bass grumblings of a surley group of gnomes, talking as they walk towards the food tables.

Glancing at the floor, I try to ignore the frolicking going on around me as I dodge an almost naked merwoman. Her green hair whips around her face and her voluptuous breasts almost come out of their seashell cups. Smiling, I hear mother's voice in my head, "stand up straight Alysium, slouching is unbecoming of a princess." Doing as she demands, I straighten my spine and raise my head, as I stare around looking for her. She has to be here somewhere, I think rolling my eyes.

"Alysium, stop being silly," her regal voice makes me jump as it comes from right behind me. How did she even find me? I think before spinning around, my lips still lifted in a smile. Her violet eyes take me in, from my braided hair, my new sky blue dress, and all the way down to the silver satin slippers poking out of the full skirt. Once she's happy with how I look, she meets my eyes.

"Mother," I greet, dipping into the small courtesy etiquette dictates. It's not as deep as those that others have to give her.

"Come now Alysium, no need for that," she tuts at me as I raise back up. "I'm glad you came, I need your help with something." She informs me, before turning and walking back the way I'd come from. Confused, I follow making sure I don't step on the ridiculous train of her rainbow dress. People move out of her path as she walks confidently to the three thrones on the dais. We're almost to the small set of steps when I notice father stood talking to a boy my own age.

His hair's dark, hanging down towards his shoulders, and from the back I can see his toned muscles through the thin black shirt that sticks to him. And mmmm, that arse is just divine! Trying to drag my eyes back up from it, I notice how his hands keep balling into fists before releasing. Who's this? My inner vixen mutters, as she likes what she sees.

"Alysium honey," Father's warm voice has my gaze shooting up, and meeting the darkest pair of eyes I've ever seen. Transfixed, I can't tear mine away, even as I feel my cheeks heat, "glad you're here." Father finishes as the boy looks away from me.

"Well not like I had much of a choice is it?" I ask sarcasm dripping from each word, as I roll my eyes making him laugh.

"Maybe not honey," he commiserates before turning to Mother, placing a kiss on her cheek.

"Alysium this is Prince Lysais," she pauses nodding towards the new boy, *"he's visiting from the Shadow World..."* what? The Shadow World? There haven't been any visitors from there since before the war began, *"...and will be staying with us at the palace for a while, so I expect you to be nice."* She continues, glaring at me, knowing that I haven't been listening.

"Ok," I mumble, glancing at Lysais, before turning back to her, waiting for her to dismiss me or give me new orders, *"so can I go now?"* I ask when she says nothing.

"Why don't you two go enjoy the party Ally," father says patiently knowing I'd rather be facing a Bellhog than remain at a court party.

"But..."

"No buts Alysium, you will escort the Prince at tonight's gathering." Mother's sharp tone leaves no room for argument, as they both turn and walk to their thrones. Leaving me with Prince Lysais and an awkward silence I don't know how to elevate.

Thankfully I don't have to, *"would you like to dance Princess?"* His soft voice makes me shiver as it breaks the silence between us. Looking at his perfectly handsome face, I struggle with my words whilst my heart races. Wow he's gorgeous, my inner vixen is fully awake now, as he watches me with those pale blue eyes.

"Ok," I answer, blushing as I place my hand in his larger one. His skin's warm, hard calluses grazing gently against my soft skin. Smiling shyly, I let him pull me slowly into the crowd, glancing back at my parents once and seeing their tight smiles and pinched eyes as I go to dance.

"You look beautiful Princess," Lysais compliments me as he tugs me around to face him, before placing one hand on my waist and raising the other, my small hand clasped within, to shoulder height. With a small smile—that makes him even more handsome—he begins to move us. Slowly at first as I stumble, staring at my feet, trying to make them remember the steps. *"Relax Princess,"* he leans

in and whispers, making me shiver.

"What?" I gasp looking up into his eyes.

"Relax, stop trying to lead," he explains, keeping my attention on him instead of my two left feet. Staring into his eyes, I let myself get lost in the shadows swimming in them as the room disappears.

"Why are you here?" I ask, flinching as my mouth blurts out exactly what I'm thinking... as it usually does.

"My mother's dying," he says simply with hardly any emotion, "and she thought it would be best if I was away from home when it happens." Watching his face I notice the slight tightening around his eyes, but other than that it's an expressionless Court mask.

"I'm so sorry," I sympathise. As much as my mother and I don't get along, I couldn't imagine life without her and to not be there to say goodbye? I can't bear to consider. Lysais dips his head in acknowledgment, before spinning us around again.

"So Princess," I really like the way he calls me Princess instead of Alysium, "why don't you like parties?" He asks, quaking his lips up in a not quite smile.

"Urg, I hate them. The dancing, the arse kissing, the deception, the lack of morals and decorum. What's there to like about them?" I ask back at him.

"Well no ones died so far," I think he mumbles under his breath before remembering where he is. "Want to get out of here?"

"Holy Aine, yes." I answer letting my manic smile take over my face. I step out of his hold and grab his hand, before tugging him after me, as we race to escape the dance floor and leave the party behind. Running through the empty halls, I laugh at the bewildered faces of the guards we surprise, as I lead Lysais outside.

Stones crunch under our feet as we hit the pebble glass walk, and I finally slow down.

"So Princess, what are we doing out here?" Lysais asks laughing.

"You'll see," I answer winking back at him.

My feet know where I'm going, even as the bright lights from the palace fade into the distance. Kicking my slippers off, I let the cool tickle of the grass soothe me, as I take Lysais to one of my most favourite places.

After five minutes, a giant hedge looms before us, making my smile bigger. Following the prickly barrier I count silently. 1, 2, 3...9,10. Reaching inside the thorns, I find the rusted handle effortlessly, and I pull it down. Glancing over my shoulder I smile at Lysais before pushing the gate open.

"We're leaving the wards princess?" he taunts, as if he thinks that will stop me.

"Scared?" I taunt back.

"Surprised, yes, scared..." he thinks about it tilting his head to one side before smirking, "no."

"Good," I say before walking through the gap in the hedge that separates the protected grounds of the palace from the meadow beyond...

"Lysais," I shout, waking with a start. Glancing around the car I gradually remember where I am.

"Dreaming again Ally?" Jace asks seriously as I notice that we've stopped.

"Yeah, where are we?"

"About 2 hours away from London." Matilda answers drawing my attention to her in the back, "who's Lysais?"

"No one." Jace and I snap together.

"Okaaay, whatever."

"Why have we stopped?" I question ignoring Matilda's tone.

"I thought you two might be hungry," my stomach decides to prove her right as it growls loudly, making them both laugh.

"Fine I can eat," I agree as I spot the golden arches of a Maccy D's, already picturing the Big Mac I'm going to devour.

"What do you fancy?" Jace asks. Turning to him I roll my eyes, like he even needs to ask, "you're right stupid question Mcdonalds it is." He answers before I can, smiling as he starts the car and turns towards the drive thru queue. One large big mac meal later, I'm happily patting my now bloated stomach as we merge back into traffic.

"So Matilda..."

"Tilly please, only my damn Sire calls me Matilda." She

interrupts.

"Fine. Tilly, what should we expect when we reach your coven?" I ask, my mind conjuring images of crypts and coffins as I turn my head to look at her.

"Not much, you'll both be staying in one of our finest hotels, near the coven but not inside it."

"Why?" I shout, surprised that she's dragged us all the way down to London, and we aren't even going to meet her mysterious coven, "what's the point of us even being here?" I ask turning fully in my seat to stare at her.

"Because it's safer to have you here, instead of running around letting loose powerful magic you can't control." She explains as if I'm stupid.

"Oh well as long as it's safer," I grumble at her, pissed off that we're wasting time coming here, "I bet you just wanted a free ride." I snark at her before slumping back in my seat and staring daggers through the front window.

"Yeah, that's it. Without you I couldn't have gotten myself back here." She snaps back, letting me know I've definitely hit a nerve.

Ignoring her, I continue staring out the window at the cars we overtake, watching the signs flash by, telling us how many miles away from London we are. I don't realise I'm drifting off until my dream continues.

"Lysais?" I ask sitting on the dew covered grass.

"Yes?"

"What's your world like?"

"It's not like here Princess that's for sure." He smiles over at me, but it doesn't reach his eyes as he glances around.

"I'd like to go there one day," I whisper to myself before flopping down on my back and staring up at the stars.

"No you wouldn't, trust me." He tells me honestly. My eyes follow the shining shape of Gallantus the Great's axe. Then Adelina with her sword pointing at her lover Byleth, the light and shadow rulers of legend.

"Their story fills me both sadness and hope." I tell Lysais as I stare

up at them.

"Whose story?" Lysais asks making me turn my head to look at him beside me brow furrowing.

"Adelina and Byleth'"

"What's their story?" He asks staring at me.

"You really don't know it, I thought Byleth was one of your ancestors?" I am intrigued.

"I know my own world's story about him," he pauses, glancing up at the stars for a moment before looking back at me, "but I'd like to hear your world's version."

"Well according to legend, Adelina was the eldest daughter of Agenia's second Queen, always lost in her own world, but a war had been raging since before she'd been born, so I suppose it must have been better in her world than ours at the time. But I'm rambling," I cut myself off with a shake of my head as he chuckles at me, and it's a wondrous sound. "Well she was kidnapped from these very palace grounds and spirited away to your world, where she faced who knows what as she never told a soul what happened there." I pause glancing at Lysais to gauge his response to my words.

"Go on," he encourages me with a smile.

"She stayed there for a year and one day, before returning home to declare that the war would be over, and that she would marry Byleth, the Shadow King's eldest son, to secure peace between our worlds." I stop not liking how the story ends.

"Sounds like a happy story why does it make you so sad?" Lysais asks, capturing a tear as it rolls down my cheek.

"Because she did stop the war but not with the marriage she had hoped for," drawing in a breath, I find the words I know by heart, "the day before their wedding, her sister was brutally murdered by the Shadow King. It broke her heart, as the marriage proposal had already been agreed and she could not escape it. Nor could she marry into the family that had killed her sweet little sister. So Adelina walked down the aisle, tears flowing down her cheeks and poison coating her lips. After they exchanged vows, she killed herself and Byleth, and with her dying words she cursed both of our families to never love each other, but to have peace for a millennia."

"That is a sad ending, but our worlds did have peace for a long time," Lysais' tone is soothing and I know he's right their deaths did accomplish peace for a time.

"But look at that peace now," I almost shouted at him as I gestured to the whole of Agenia, *"I've never known peace in my lifetime, have you?"*

I knew from the sad look in his eyes that he hasn't either, the war between our worlds erupted before either of us had been born and has raged ever since.

"Ally?" Jace's voice breaks up the dream/memory, whatever the fuck it was as I feel a tear roll down my cheek.

"Yeah?" I groggily acknowledge him, with a hiccup.

"We're here, sleepy head," Jace laughs as I rub the sleep from my eyes.

"I didn't know women snored, until now," Tilly snorted from the back seat.

Chapter Twelve

Alyssa.

We'd been at this godforsaken hotel in some deserted part of London for days, and I'm beginning to go stir crazy staring at the same four walls. We're getting nowhere just sitting here waiting for Tilly's vampire coven to make some decision. "Damn Vampires," I growled at the empty room. The urge to break something rises in me as I spot the heavy looking vase. Picking it up, I draw my hand back as the door inches open.

"What's that Ally?" Jace's bored tone reaches me as he appraises the vase in my hand, "and what are you planning for that poor vase?" He jokes with a teasing smile that makes me huff out a laugh.

"It's going against that wall," I answer letting my frustration show.

"Come on Ally, we both know you're not going to smash something that's not yours."

My anger deflates at his words, and my arm holding the vase lowers. He's right. I'd never break someone else's property, I don't even know why I'd thought about smashing it in the first place. My emotions have been going haywire for days, and being cooped up inside hasn't helped.

Tilly explained that we were now in Hampstead Garden Suburbs, aka Vampire territory. Her coven protects and enforces all vampire laws in the UK. She also explained that a few small groups of other, what they called, suppers lived here, in what the humans thought were abandoned and decaying mansions. But the vampire's owned everything, even the beautiful—if old style —hotel we're currently staying in.

Tilly had secured us a room each and then disappeared, stating that she needed to check in on the council and her hunters. And we'd only seen her once again since, when she'd informed us about a young witch that one of her huntresses had found in

York, who might be able to help us find Lilah, if we'd be willing to help her. But since then, we've heard no more.

After that meeting I'd not left my room, too afraid to leave in case my magic decided to show itself or I missed Tilly coming again. Feeling like a prisoner, I drop on to the ridiculously comfy sofa and stare daggers at Jace as he saunters across the room to me.

"What's got you so worked up?" He asks knowing the damn answer before I speak.

"Why are we sitting around here waiting Jace?" I ask back.

"Because we need the help," I know he's right, but I hate waiting. My mind keeps thinking what Lilah could be going through without us. She might have tried to find us in York by now, might be going out of her mind not knowing where we are.

"We should be looking for Lilah not sitting around here waiting on strangers," I grumble, picking absently at a loose thread on my top.

"We don't even know where to start Ally," he begins, but I tune him out as I hear a noise in the hallway outside my door. My hearing has been getting stronger over the last few days, and it's annoying as hell! No one ever tells you how much getting superpowers sucks. When you can hear every tiny noise through the walls, every argument, conversation, action that happens behind closed doors. My head feels like it's going to burst at any moment. I need to figure out how to turn it off.

"What the hell is with all this..." I try to ask before my door slams into the wall and a very, very angry vampire is leaning over me.

"What the fuck are you doing here?" The angry vampire hisses right into my face, as I try to place hers, I'm pretty sure I know her from somewhere? But where? I wonder watching her face closely.

"...waiting." I finish my sentence, as she leans closer, growing I continue letting my boredom shine through in my voice, "we've been here for days now," I explain. Then it hits me, she's the vampire, the huntress from next to the river.

"For what?" She snarls inching closer still.

"For Tilly," I state back, not letting her intimidate me.

"Ladies," Jace interjects, drawing both of our attention to him.

"Stay out of this Jace," I growled.

As the huntress growls, "what?" I watch as Jace's face pales, before he holds up his hands in surrender and walks to the door. "I'll leave you to it, just don't destroy the room," he says, glancing over his shoulder before leaving and shutting the door behind him.

"Who the hell are you?" I shout at her, leaning a little closer.

"Dina," she states distractedly before asking, "how do you know Tilly?" in a slightly less angry tone as she moves out of my personal space.

"She found us, not the other way around and I don't really know her." I concede.

"What did you do?" Dina accuses, raising my hackles again.

"Nothing!" I shout at her, then remember the blast of magic I let loose in the park, "well I might have used magic."

"What the fuck," she mumbles running a hand through her short hair, "just who the fuck are you?"

I shrug because, as of right now, I have no idea who the hell I am, or what the hell I am. Feeling the need to pace, I push up from the sofa and walk to the window. Life outside carries on, people are shopping, or hurrying past to work, everything looks normal. If you can ignore the odd clueless human that doesn't see the beautiful buildings they're blindly taking photographs of. "How do you keep it all from them?" I ask intrigued not for the first time that the humans see rotting, derelict buildings, so completely different to what we see.

"What?" Dina asks, confused at my sudden switch in topic.

"The humans. All they see are run down mansions, how do you do it?"

"Witches," Dina states like it should be obvious, "you really are clueless aren't you." She groans again, running her hand through her short hair in frustration.

"Guess I am." I answer sarcastically, returning my gaze to the street outside and letting loose a sigh. "I have no idea who I really am, I dream of fantastical things, I can shoot elements from my hands...well sometimes I can," I complain, staring at my now normal looking hands. "All of you seem to know more about me than I do, but none of you can tell me anything without hurting me." I look over my shoulder at her as my words sink in. "Can you imagine how that feels?" I ask, needing just one person who understands how screwed up my head is right now. "Of course you don't," I scoff, answering for her when she remains silent.

After what feels like hours I hear the soft pad of her feet, as Dina begins pacing the room behind me. Shaking my head I try to ignore both her and the many questions running around my head. "When will Tilly be back?" I ask spinning around and pinning my frown on Dina where she's pacing a hole into the carpet. One look at her and I can tell she's just as sick of this bloody waiting as I am.

"When she is," She answers, waving her hand through the air without breaking her stride, as if waiting on Tilly is a normal thing worth no more than a second of consideration. "Why?"

"Because I need answers," I try not to give too much away, not ready to trust these vampires, even if they have been nice to us so far. Looking around the hotel room I wonder again why we're even here. "You know what I am," I state, meeting her dark eyes.

"Yes."

"You know I don't."

"Yes."

"I need help." I whisper, sick of her one word answers. "Tilly says there's a young witch that might be able to help." Dina nods but says nothing, her face an unreadable mask. I wait as patiently as I can for her to say something, anything else.

"Tilly always says too much," she growls lowly, "but I'm sorry we can't help you," Dina says before turning to the door, our conversation apparently over.

Anger surges through my veins at her apparent lack of giving a shit. I feel heat travel down my arms as Dina takes another step towards the door. My fingers tingle, and I can't keep it in, as my rage boils to the surface and flames suddenly block her from touching the door as my voice shouts, "Can't or won't!?"

"Can't." Dina says firmly as I blink, and she's right in front of my face, rage contorting hers, "Charleene can't control her emerging powers, so she can't help you with whatever you need her for." It's the most I've ever heard her say in one go. "She's got enough to worry about without your problems as well!" My anger gives one last roar at her words the flames blocking the door leaping higher, "I won't let you hurt her," Dina whispers darkly, deflating what's left of my anger and taking my conjured fire with it, leaving nothing but a scorched black mark on the fancy carpet.

Turning back to the window, I feel defeated as I let Dina's words sink in. *So that's it,* I think to myself. "No-one will help us." I whisper to myself, as tears drop down my cheek. My mind spins out of control, filled with thoughts of Lilah being held hostage or demons ripping apart the few people I actually care about, or how I'll never know what the hell I am.

"Well I didn't say that now did I?" Dina's calm voice interrupts my dark thoughts, making me realise I'd said them all out loud.

"What?" I ask cautiously, trying not to let her words ignite a small beacon of hope in me, that had just died. Turning slowly I wait for her to say more.

"We're going to search for Charleene's Coven," Dina pauses staring at me as though she's going to regret what she's about to say, "you're coming with us," she says with a sigh before letting herself out the suit door, "be ready at 8am." And then she's gone, as I stand bewildered just staring at the door.

I'm frozen in shock, staring at the dark wood as it pushes open a few minutes later, "soooo the rooms still standing," Jace jokes before seeing the black scorch mark on the floor as he walks into my room, "well almost," he states looking at me sceptically, "you?"

Nodding, I hang my head in shame, annoyed that I'd let my magic and my anger get the better of me again. Beating myself up again at the strange things that keep happening to me. All

I want is to find Lilah and understand what's happening, and why. I'd just got my head around the last few times and now apparently I have to add fire to the mix as well.

Great, just great Ally you're a fucking accident waiting to happen, I scold myself. *What the fuck is wrong with me?* Each time I sleep more memories come, but they don't actually answer any of my questions. It's frustrating to say the least, is it too hard to ask for just one memory about my magic?

"What's going on in that head of yours Ally?" Jace asks, breaking into my spiraling dark thoughts.

"Nothing," I answer honestly because nothing good is going on inside my head, "I'm just frustrated Jace, I want to know what's going on with me." I sigh.

"I know you do Ally and as soon as we can figure out how to remove the block on your mind everything will be easier." Jace explains patiently.

"What block?" I ask accusingly. This is the first time I'm hearing about any damn block. I know Jace knows more than he's been telling me, and it's starting to really grate on my nerves. Who am I supposed to trust if even my best friend won't tell me the truth. "Jace, you'd better tell me what the hell is going on."

"Come on Ally, you know that's not fair," Jace groans, running his hands through his already messy hair.

"No Jace I've had enough, either you tell me or I walk out this door and never come back." I threaten.

"And go where Ally?" He asks, calling my bluff.

"I don't know. Anywhere but here Jace!" I shout in frustration at him, as the last word is screamed I find myself no longer in my hotel room but standing in a beautiful garden instead.

"Why won't you believe me, Jacin?" I shout, he's always had my back, always trusted me to know myself, and that I can trust my gut.

"Because you can't see it Ally!" Jace spits back at me, nudging my temper, raising it higher.

"See what exactly?" I ask.

"That he's using you Ally, he has been since he met you," he's *frustrated with how close me and Ly have been getting recently. Just like everyone else, he doesn't trust him.*

"I know he's from Penumbra, but not everyone's the same as the Shadow King you know," I *fling at him before turning on my heel. I need to get away from Jacin before one of us says something we'll regret.*

"Now where are you going?"

"Anywhere but here Jacin!" I *scream at him, flinging my arms in the air in frustration.*

And as quick as the memory came it's gone, leaving me speechless as I stare at Jace. "Jacin, just who are you?" I ask, knowing I need to hear it from him. I need to know if we were more than just friends before whatever happened to me. I watch as he grapples with his head and his heart. "Please tell me?" I whisper sick of fighting already.

"My true name is Jacin and I'm your protector Ally, always have been and always will be." He's being honest with me, even if I won't fully understand the importance of what he's saying.

"Was that all we were?" His flinch makes me frown as I watch him.

"Yes." He answers quickly, as if he's scared that one of his answers will hurt me again.

"And what did you have to protect me from?" I ask curious.

"Everything," he sighs. "Even yourself sometimes," he adds, his lips tilting up in the smallest of smiles as if he's remembering doing just that.

"Must have been hard," I mutter, making him laugh.

"Extremely."

"And this block was to protect me?" I ask, wanting to keep him talking.

"Yes," he whispers back acknowledging my correct thoughts.

"And you placed it on me?" I ask even knowing somehow that he didn't do this to me.

"No, it wasn't me Ally," he says, shaking his head, his eyes filled with sadness.

"Who did this to me, Jace?"

He opens his mouth before shutting it again, clearly torn between answering me and not. "What did you remember Ally?" He asks, taking me by surprise.

Moving to the sofa I sit down and make myself comfortable, waiting until he joins me before I launch in to everything I've remembered so far. I tell him about the strange man's voice, about the balls with the weird creatures. I explain about remembering Lysias, making him frown as I smile. I tell him what I remember of him, about his pointy ears and that black jacket with silver swirls. Once I'm finished Jace just stares at me in disbelief.

"Those are earlier memories Ally, mostly from your childhood," he explains, giving me a time frame for the disjointed memories.

"Ok, so how old was I when this happened to me?" I ask gesturing at myself.

"Fifteen in human years," he says and I know he's just choosing a comparison that I'll understand.

"And what are we really?" I ask, instinctively knowing I can handle the answer.

"Fae Ally, we are Fae," he says softly, watching me carefully for any signs that he's triggered the block.

"Like Fairies?" I ask, not quite believing him, "little beings with wings, that glow?" I question wondering if he's gone mental as well as me.

"Little no, wings yes, and some of us glowed but not all," he answers seriously.

"Okaaay," I respond with my eyebrows climbing to my hairline, as I try to contain my laughter. *I'm a fairy, yeah right.* I think to myself trying to imagine myself with wings and a little bag of fairy dust like in Peter Pan.

"It's not funny Alysium," he says trying not to laugh with me, as I sober up from my hysterics enough to realise he's just called me by the name from my dreams/memories whatever they were.

"Ally huh?" I question him, making him squirm. He opens his mouth to say something but I beat him to it, "short for Alysium right?" I confirm.

"Yeah. It feels good to be able to tell you this much," he says, relief clear on his face.

"That's going to take some getting used to," I mock, shoving him with my foot, making him lose his balance and almost end up on the floor. Which causes us both to crack up laughing, when the door opens again.

"Did I miss something?" Tilly's voice rings across the room making us laugh even harder at her confused face. "Ok it's official you're both crazy." She declares before joining us, and sitting on the floor to wait out our hysterics. "So I hear Adrina came to see you," Tilly states when our giggle fit subsides and I feel lighter than I have in a while.

"Who?" I ask.

"Oh yeah, what did the other vamp want?" Jace asks at the same time, clueing me in to who Tilly was talking about.

"Dina," Tilly clarifies.

"Oh yeah, she said they couldn't help me," I explained to them both, "but that we can join them in looking for Charleene's coven." I say before either of them can ask me any questions.

"Ah yes, the ever elusive Scottish Coven." Tilly agrees.

"What do you mean elusive?" Jace asks his brow furrowing as he watches Tilly closely.

"They've not been heard from in years. It's a wonder that Charleene is even part of their coven as they normally don't lose their children." Tilly says matter of factly like losing a child is no big thing.

"How do you lose a child?" I ask bewildered. Surely parents always know where their kids are. Tilly just shrugs as though the answer isn't important.

"The only reason we know she belongs to them is because one of the elders knew one of her relatives. She's apparently the spitting image of her ancestor."

"What do you know about them then, if you don't know where they are?" Jace asks getting down to the things he deems important.

"We know they are still somewhere in Scotland, just not exactly where. We heard whispers about 19 years ago that they were attacked and went into hiding and that's about it." She says meeting both of our eyes.

"So what do we do just search the whole of Scotland, do you know how big it is?" I ask sarcastically.

"No dufus, you take Charleene, all witches have an inherited bond with their coven, once you're close enough she should be able to tell. Dina will also be checking in with sources she has up there to see if they know anything."

Now that she'd explained those key pieces of information, my sense of dread lifted a little. "And her coven might be able to help me?" I ask skeptical.

"Definitely, they're the most powerful coven we have in the UK."

"Good," I answered. I'll get some answers hopefully at some-point.

"Yeah, because the Elders aren't too happy that there are three ancients running around unchecked." Tilly explains before telling us what else was said at the council meeting she'd been in for the last few days. Including the reason her and Dina were in York, the link between the missing and murdered girls. Apparently the vampire's like to know what's going on in the UK and finding out that we've been here for years without their knowledge has pissed them off. "So they want you both to find the coven so you can go home." She finishes as we both stare at her.

"Well those murders have nothing to do with us." Jace exclaims when she's done.

"We know, a rogue Vampire has been killing them, from what Dina found out he's been hunting and killing witches before their powers manifest."

"Why?" I ask before I can stop myself as that night under the bridge makes more sense.

"We don't know," Tilly answers honestly, "but we're afraid that he's going to be hunting Charleene since she escaped him."

"Great so we'll have a sadistic vampire killer after us as well as those shadow people things."I huff wondering—not for the first time—how my life got so messed up.

"Demoran," Jace interjects, confusing the hell out of me.

"What?" Tilly and I both ask together, staring at Jace.

"Demoran, that's what the shadow men are called."

"What the hell is a De-mor-an?" Tilly asks, sounding out the name.

"Creatures created by the Shadow King, we don't know if they're alive or dead or somewhere in-between." He explains to us both slowly, "they're made of shadows and can only be killed with magic or taking off their heads."

"Great, just great," I mutter to myself, as I realise the danger we'll be putting everyone in if we go with them. "I know I need to get this block removed but there must be another way." I implore both of them not willing to endanger others.

"I don't think there is Ally," Jace tries to reassure me, as my panic rises at the thought of others being hurt because of me.

"They're already in danger Ally," Tilly reminds me as I shake my head at them. "Look, just sleep on it ok?"

I nod my agreement, but I already know no matter how much sleep I get my mind won't change and, from the slight twist of Jace's lips, he knows as well.

"Good. Then we'll all meet here in the morning to go over the whole plan and raise any concerns."

"Will you be coming with us?" I ask hopefully as I realise she's growing on me a little.

"No," Tilly dashes my hope before it even fully rises in me, but she must see the disappointment on my face as she adds, "I have other matters to attend to, but I'm sure our paths will cross again."

"Ok," I say with a small smile, before she leaves us alone to mull over everything.

"What are we going to do?" I ask turning to Jace as the door closes behind Tilly.

"What do you mean Ally?" He asks back, frowning as if my question was confusing.

"About everything, we can't put them in danger," I tell him, speaking my mind, "it's not fair." I say in frustration at our situation.

"Ally calm down," Jace mutters, watching my hands warily where they're gripping the sofa, "before you set something else on fire."

His joke sobers me quickly as I reign my emotions in, yeah that's right I can't get emotional nowadays I snark silently in my head. Lumping backwards in defeat I let go of any remaining hope that I can just be a normal girl, that this was all some mistake a delusion I'd created.

Chapter Thirteen

Jacin.

Bloody hell. I thought, leaving Alyssa alone to process everything we'd just heard. She'd almost burnt the whole suite down, just because she was pissed off. If this was a sign of things to come, I wasn't holding out hope that we'd make it to Lilah before Ally set Dina on fire. Letting out a chuckle, I pictured the rage on Dina's face as Alyssa had stopped her from leaving. Princess Alysium was awakening, slowly but surely, thanks to that no good son of a bitch turning up and it was terrifying.

We'd known that the weaving her Father had placed on her wouldn't last forever as her own magic would attack it, but King Halsper had thought, hoped, it would take longer than three years. Lysais' presence in this world was a cluster fuck of epic proportions, and that damn mating bond would be a bugger to hide but I needed to find a way.

"Fuck," I muttered shutting the door to my own suite behind me, "where have you gone Lilah? I bloody need you." I raged at the empty room as I let my frustration over everything slip out. I needed Lilah more than ever and she'd be disappointed. We'd planned for everything but this one eventuality, how stupid we'd both been. Thinking he wouldn't find her here. After the first year of being safe we'd grown lax in our precautions, and then another year passed much the same so we moved around a little less, until I'd even convinced Lilah that we could go to the human's university, allowing Ally to live a more human life.

Stupid, stupid, stupid. I silently berated myself again for the millionth time. How had I not noticed the signs before that Bastard had shown up. Fuck knows when Ally had stopped taking the pills Lilah concocted, to keep her memories murky and hidden as dreams. The magic binding her had been weakening the whole time we'd been in York, and I'd missed it. Some protector I'd been, caught up in the fantasy that we were just normal students.

I'd hated lying to Ally all this time, but at least with Lilah being the voice of reason, I'd been able to squash the doubts of this being the right way to protect her. She was my princess, even if she didn't remember right now, and it was my job to protect her. But fuck me! If this lying had to go any longer, I don't know what would happen to our friendship, she was too important for me to lose her. I just had to hope that she'd eventually understand.

We needed to find Lilah, she'd know how to fix this mess. And I needed to find a way to keep Lysais the fuck away from Ally, because it was clear the bond was already drawing her to him. After the atrocities he'd committed the last time they'd been together on Agenia, he didn't deserve to breathe the same air as Alysium.

I needed to find Tilly. Maybe she'd know some way to protect Ally from her own heart until she remembered everything.

Chapter Fourteen

Alyssa.

"Urggg! Knock it off!" I shouted, pushing my head from beneath my quilt as the incessant knocking continues, dragging me out of one of the best dreams so far. No creatures, balls, training sessions, just me and Lysias laying on a warm beach as the waves tickle our toes.

Allowing myself to smile for a few seconds, I give in and finally let myself fully wake up, but whoever's at that damn door is going to get a piece of my mind. Grabbing one of the fluffy white hotel robes, I put it on over my shorts and tank top before opening the bedroom door and walking across the living area, to the door that's rattling on its hinges as another round of knocking starts up.

Flipping the lock off I swing the door open, my mouth open, ready to unleash hell on the person before me. "What bloody time do you call this?" I shout at the plain looking girl standing before me, as my mind registers her smile falling from her face.

"Erm..." the girl says, flinching away from me and my anger, "I thought you might like some coffee?" She rushes out so quickly that the words all run together in a quiet voice.

Her deep blue eyes leave mine, looking down at the floor, as her thin fingers incessantly tap against the paper cup clutched in her hand. "Oh," I grumble, feeling guilty for shouting at her. I thought it would be Jace or Dina, not the lass from the bridge, "sorry" I mutter.

"It's ok, it is early," she mumbles to the floor before meeting my gaze, "I'm Charleene, we met in York briefly." She explains with a shy smile, "Dina says you're coming with us today?" I can't tell if she's asking a question, or just stating a fact, as she fidgets in the hall.

"I guess we are," I say smiling at her, "is coffee still an option?" I ask wanting to put her at ease after scaring her. Smiling, she nods and holds out the cup to me.

"I didn't know how you take it, so I brought milk and sugar." She says, already digging through her coat pockets, as I move away from the door.

"Come in," I tell her sniffing at the caffeinated goodness she's given me, "Jace should arrive soon," I explain as she closes the door behind her.

"Yeah he said as much when I gave him his cup," she says blushing scarlet, telling me that he obviously wasn't wearing much when he answered the door.

"It's ok you know, he has that effect on all women," I say conspiratorially, my smile widening as she blushes more.

"It's not that, I'm not..." She stutters clearly embarrassed, before letting it go and sitting down, as she finally finds a mountain of sugar packets and milk cartons.

"What did you do, steal all their condiments?" I joke as she deposits them on the small table, gaining a snort of a laugh from her.

"Maybe," she agrees, slipping out of her coat, giving me a look at her t-shirt, and I can't help laughing. Fuck this life, it read, which I whole heartedly agreed with right now. Charleene looked conflicted for a moment before blurting out what's on her mind "Dina says your Fae?" She gets out, before slamming her hand against her mouth, "sorry I shouldn't have said that." She apologises before I can say anything.

"It's ok and yes apparently I am." I tell her liking her already.

"Apparently?" She questions picking up on my uncertainty.

"I don't really remember being anything other than human," I explain.

"You look human, no pointy ears or wings," she says looking around me at my back, "unless you're hiding them." She muses to herself as her eyes return to my face.

"Not that I know of," I smile back at her, liking her even more. "And you're a witch?" I ask back, trying to see anything out of the ordinary about her, but she looks human enough sitting there. Her long blonde hair drifting in waves over her shoulders, tight black jeans with frayed holes letting her tanned skin poke through and killer rainbow hightop trainers.

"Apparently I am," she repeats my words back at me, making me wonder just what her story is. "I mean I've used magic once but that's completely new to me and..."

"Scary," we both say at the same time, before bursting out laughing. We're still trying to contain our giggles when the others walk into my room, and find us both hunched over holding our sides.

"Well looks like you two are going to be great friends," Jace states before shoving me over and sitting next to me.

"Great," Dina exclaims before perching on the coffee table, her gaze softening slightly as she looks over at Charleene, *hmmm is that worry in her eyes?* I think to myself before her gaze moves to me and her familiar scowl returns.

"When do we leave?" I find myself asking to fill the silence, my gaze bouncing between Dina and Tilly.

"In an hour, we can take your car." Dina answers in a business-like tone, as she takes control of us all. Watching me and Jace carefully, she opens her mouth to add something before thinking better of it.

"What?" I sigh.

"Nothing, you should get your things together," she says instead, before looking at Jace, "you too blondie."

Smirking, "I'm all packed Beautiful," Jace says confidently, fixing Dina with his pantie-melting smile and, for what must be the first time ever, I watch as it fails. Dina's face doesn't change, she doesn't soften towards him like every woman normally does. It's all I can do not to burst out laughing at the confusion I see in his eyes as he looks at Dina.

"You're wasting your time on that one," Tilly giggles, flicking her green eyes at Dina, pausing halfway out of my seat. I watch Jace, waiting for him to figure it out and it's worth it. I watch as his brow smooths out, and he flicks his eyes to Charleene and back to Dina as the penny drops, he doesn't lose the smile though, as he relaxes back into the sofa.

"Good to know," Jace says, showing respect in his tone, "Ally you just going to stand there, or actually go get packed and ready?" He asks drawing everyone's attention back to me, great.

"Yeah, won't be long." I say, already backing towards the bedroom, leaving them to talk through everything I can't hear yet. I hate being in the dark, I grumble in my head as I close the wooden door behind me, and head over to the small wardrobe where my meager selection of clothes hang. Letting out a sigh at being excluded, I grab my brown leather bag from the top, and start packing away the clothes I brought with me.

Chewing my lip nervously, I glance at the still closed door before deciding to grab a shower. I let myself enjoy the warm water as it almost scolds, turning my skin pink as it works out all the tension from my shoulders. Smiling, I use some of my favourite apple scented shampoo and conditioner. When I finally feel clean and relaxed, I shut the water off and get dressed into my comfiest blue jeans, soft yellow t-shirt and pink fluffy socks. *Perfect clothes for traveling in,* I think to myself, before checking all the draws to make sure I've not missed anything.

Bracing myself emotionally for whatever is about to happen, I throw the strap of my bag over my shoulder, and breathe deeply before pushing open the door to the muted voices of the others. Shivers run over my body as I remind myself they're not excluding me on purpose, as my gaze locks onto Jace. He's been keeping things from me for the last three years, for "my safety" as he's been reminding me.

Everyone stops talking as I come out of my room and all eyes are on me as I walk towards them. "So where are we going first?" I ask to fill the silence.

"Scotland." Charleene's quiet voice answers.

"Ok," I put as much confidence into my voice as I can as I looked from face to face, "when do we leave?"

"Now, if you're ready," says Dina.

I nod once before walking to the door, "and how long is it to Edinburgh?" I ask as we walk down the fancy hallway.

"About eight hours," Dina answers quickly.

"That's a long drive," I state thinking of how numb my bum is going to be.

"We'll have breaks," Charleene mutters with a hint of uncertainty colouring her voice, as though even she isn't sure that we'll actually stop.

"Sure," Dina's voice sounds kinder when she speaks to Charleene and I once again wonder what is going on between the two of them.

"And what's in Edinburgh?" Jace asks before I can.

"Hopefully information," Tilly explains.

"And how does this help us find Lilah exactly?" I ask, the pit of worry in my stomach growing.

"Once we've found the coven, we can ask them to scry for her." Dina states.

"And why would this coven help us? It's not like they know us." I point out.

"Trust me, everyone wants your kind gone from earth," Dina grumbles.

"Why?" I ask, just as we reach the glass elevator. *This hotel really is very nice*, I think Tilly mentioned that it was 5 star when we arrived.

"Because you cause trouble," Dina grumbles as I push the call button. I open my mouth to defend us but then, thinking back on everything that's happened lately, I realise I can't argue against her statement. Between my erratic magic and the Demoran showing up we really have caused trouble.

I'm still mulling over everything as we step into the lift and it descends silently to the lobby. None of us talk as we walk through the busy reception area. Dina peels off and goes over to the desk as the rest of us step out into blinding sunshine. My eyes are still adjusting when a young lad drives Jace's car to a stop in front of us. "My baby," Jace grins as the valet puts his keys in his hand.

Shaking my head, I open the boot and throw my small bag on top of everything else that's crammed inside. "What's the matter?" Charleene's voice makes me jump as it comes from right behind me.

"Nothing" I mutter flashing her a small smile before going to the front passenger seat and climbing in as Dina leaves the hotel carrying two suitcases.

"Take care of yourself," Tilly says, blocking my window as she leans in and fixes me with a stern stare.

"I will," I find myself promising her, "Will we see you again?" I ask knowing this could be the last time we see her.

"Possibly," She answers cryptically with a shrug and a smile, before turning and clasping forearms with Dina.

"You Ok Ally?" Jace asks, drawing my attention to his worried gaze.

"I will be," I answer honestly, as the back doors slam shut and Jace puts the car into gear. Then we're slowly pulling away from the curb, glancing in the wing mirror I let out a chuckle at Tilly waving us off like a mad woman. I really like her, I realise as we leave her behind.

A tug in my body lets me know when we drive over the invisible barrier that keeps Hampsted gardens secret from the humans of London. I let out the breath I've been holding. I stop looking behind us and stare at the road before us. London to Edinburgh. What a trip! Over eight hours if we do it on one long drive, eight and a half hours with a vampire, a witch and two Fae stuck in a car together. What a combination I joke to myself as the road before us flashes past, my arse is going to be killing by the time we reach Edinburgh. God knows how this journey will end, but at least we're finally doing something.

"So what powers do you have?" Dina pipes up from the back seat behind me, making me jump as she drags me from my thoughts.

"Um I dunno," I answer honestly shrugging.

"Well we know you have fire and you mentioned something about air at the hotel," she snorts, trying to smother a laugh as I glare over my shoulder at her. "What else have you used?"

"Alyssa has loads of powers," Jacin answers before I can, "She's been trained in all types of combat, magical and physical." We all stare at him as he drives with a smug smirk on his face, "she just doesn't remember any of it." He adds reluctantly.

"Well that's helpful," Dina remarks.

"She just needs to train, it's more than your defective witch can do" Jace remarks back, just as snippy as Dina was.

"She needs to learn that's all," Dina snipes back defensively, "Charleene's had no training, it's not like she was made to forget." Dina fires back making me feel an inch tall as my head goes back and forth between Jace and her.

"And Ally just needs to train," Jace states confidently as I gape

"Just like I do?" Charleene suddenly interrupts the argument, gaining all of our attention. "I need to learn how to protect myself." She states to us, her voice hopeful as she meets each of our gazes. Running my eyes up and down her I notice how delicate she is, like a strong wind would be enough to blow her over. I couldn't picture her protecting herself, fighting even, and then I remember the Vampire from near the river. She has dangerous enemies too, just like me, so why shouldn't she learn how to fight.

"Damn right you do." I state, drawing the angriest glare from Dina that I'd ever seen, "what? She needs to learn about herself as much as I do, you won't always be there to protect her." I state meeting her icy glare and not backing down. I watch as my words sink in through Dina's urge to protect Charleene.

"Fine!" Dina reluctantly agrees as Charleene lets out a very girly high pitched squeal, "So how's this going to work? Where would we even train them both?" Dina asks the back of Jace's head like he would know the answer.

"They'd need to be protected, but I don't think we can afford to wait. What about your...friends?" Jace asks sceptically, meeting Dina's eyes in the mirror.

"Will He be able to find me again?" I find myself asking, not able to help myself as Ly's face flashes in my mind. Do I want him to find me? I wonder as my heart begins to race. I know Jace doesn't like him but there's something between us, something that I'm finding it harder to deny to myself.

"No, at least I don't think so." Jace mumbles so quietly that I would have missed it before.

"What have you done Jace?" I ask cautiously.

"Protected you." He answers, glancing at my face and back to the road.

"What if I don't want protecting from him?"

"Tough, you don't want him around Ally, he's not good for you."

"That's my decision to make not yours!" I state flatly, glaring at the side of his head.

"No it's not, you can't be trusted when it comes to Him!" Jace responds just as flatly.

"Who's He?" Charleene's voice interrupts us before my anger can grow further.

"No one!" We both snarl back at her, before lapsing into silence as I glare out the side window, watching the motorway flash past.

"Okaaay," I hear Charleene mutter softly.

Fuming I watch as we speed past car after car. *He can't be that bad can he?* I think, as I try forcing myself to remember anything more. I know I should trust Jace, but after everything recently it's hard to trust anything, even my own feelings apparently. Frustrated, I glance at Jace, tracing his face with my eyes, reconciling the Jace I know and love with the Jace from my dreams with the pointed ears.

"The lady from my dreams, she's my mum isn't she?" I find myself asking, breaking the silence.

"Yes," Jace's voice is tight as he briefly glances my way.

"What happened to her?"

"I don't know Ally," the sadness in his eyes tells me he's telling the truth.

"She was scared for me, I mean in all the memories I've had of her, her eyes are filled with fear when they look at me..." I pause not knowing if I want the answer to the question burning in my head. Taking a deep breath I plunge ahead, "Jace, am I dangerous? Did I hurt people?"

"What?" Jace looks at me then, stares out at the road for a few seconds before shaking his head, "no Ally! You hurt no one, your parents were scared for you, not of you."

Meeting his eyes, I let silence reign again in the car thinking over his answer, I'd not hurt anyone but someone clearly had been hurt. Why would my parents be scared for me, what had been going on? And why had everyone thought it best that I remember nothing? Frustrated and angry at ghosts I never knew had been haunting me, I found myself drifting off, as Dina's sharp voice filled the car.

"What the hell?" She snaps, making my head snap around to glare at her. She's looking down at the caller I.d, before swiping her thumb across the display and answering, "what's going on?" She snaps just as gruffly at the person on the other end. All of our heads snap towards Dina and the voice coming from her phone as a lady's voice speaks. "Ok, we'll be careful, thank you for letting me know, I will, bye." The one sided conversation has us all waiting for more, especially as Dina's poker face reveals nothing.

"Who was it?" Charleene asks, her eyes wide enough that even I could see the small flecks of gold clearly.

"No one important," Dina answers quickly, reaching out to caress Charleene's face, trying to calm her down.

"Don't lie to me Dina, I'm not a child," Charleene states, pushing away as much as she can in the small confines of the car.

Letting out a sigh, I watch as Dina weighs up her options before, sighing again clearly frustrated with the news she's just received, "the hunter has moved away from York, it looks like he's stalking you Charleene." She growls the last few words so fast I almost miss them.

"Who?" Jace asks, confused as he glances between the road and the rear view mirror.

"The vampire from under the bridge?" I question at the same time, watching as Charleene's face drains of colour.

"How?" She whispers, her frightened eyes not leaving Dina's.

"We don't know, he must have help," Dina states, clearly

thinking of her prey instead of the scared girl sitting beside her. Looking at Charleene, I'm sure she's going to either burst into tears or piss herself. Reaching back, I squeeze her leg as Dina rattles off different supernatural species that could be helping the sadistic Vampire under her breath. It's like she's trying to figure out the whole puzzle with only a handful of the pieces.

"Why?" Charleene interrupts Dina's monologue drawing all of our attention to her, "Who am I to be worth all of this trouble and effort?"

"We're going to find out babe." Dina states, grabbing her hand and squeezing, "the coven thinks you're powerful, maybe that's why he's after you?"

"What if he catches me before we find the Scottish coven?" Charleene whispers brokenly.

"I won't let that happen!" Dina states protectively.

"But what if?" Charleene asks again on a sob.

"Ssshhhh, I'll die before I let that bastard touch you," Dina declares, brushing the tears from Charleene's cheeks, and from the venom in her voice, I believe her.

"We'll help too," I find myself promising with a quick glance at Jace's face. At his small nod I know I speak for the pair of us. "And you'll be able to protect yourself before long," I announced brightly, trying to cheer her up as she meets my eyes. "Jace will knock us both into shape." I smile at her.

"Damn right I will," Jace confirms confidently, making her smile.

"And I have contacts up in Scotland who can help hide us and look for your Coven," Dina states, making Charleene's shoulders relax further into the car seat.

"Hey it could be worse," I find myself saying.

"How?" Charleene whispers, meeting my eyes confused.

"You could be in love with the man hunting you," I say mindlessly, before realising what I've just let slip in front of Jace.

"That's true, is that what's happening to you?" She asks, gaining a little colour back into her cheeks, as I nod with a small smile.

"You don't love him Ally," Jace states his disapproval clear, "you don't know him. If you did you'd hate him." From the finality in his voice I knew Jace won't be speaking about this particular topic again with me.

"Maybe," I agree to keep the peace, as my mind returns to the memories I have of my shadow lord. Since coming into my life he'd done nothing but protect me, yet if Jace is to be believed he can't be trusted—like his note said—no it's worse than that, he wants to hurt me? Confused doesn't even begin to cover what I feel right now, why couldn't my life have just stayed as it was?

Frustrated, I glance around at my unlikely companions, noting how Charleene looks scared to death, while Dina has what I'm going to call her stabby face on and Jace, well he just looks like he always does confident and cocky as he drives us closer to Scotland and hopefully answers.

Chapter Fifteen

Lysais.

He hadn't noticed when I'd silenced the bond, I'd managed to hide it from him but then this morning he'd felt his damn tracking spell unravel. "You fucking idiot," He snarled at me, throwing whatever came to hand at the wall opposite us. "We have no way to find her now!" He raged letting himself feel his burning anger as I just laughed silently.

She's safe now. I taunted, fuck him for thinking he was so clever.

"No. She'll never be safe, you idiot! Don't you get it, if we don't find her, then someone else will," he threw back at me, making my need to protect her rise up, as I rattled my cage, almost frothing at the mouth when he just tightened his hold on me.

My memories came on hard and fast as he removed the barrier keeping them from me. *Small breathy gasps* fill my mind, *as my gaze roams over her perfect skin as if she was right in front of me. My lips and tongue felt warm as it glided over her flesh as I closed in on her pert, pale nipple.*

Then just as fast I'm back in the room staring into his cold sneering eyes, "you bastard," I curse at him as he uses my own mind against me.

"And what do you think someone else will do to her?" He snaps at me, making me flinch backwards. "I wouldn't touch her, violate her, but someone else would."

I'm so enraged by his words, I hadn't considered that there would be others out looking for her. Others that might do exactly what Balor said, *Fuck!* I yell inside my mind. Trying to find anyway to break this fucking mind bond.

No one got to touch her like that, I'd kill them if they tried putting one finger on her!

Chapter Sixteen

Alyssa.

Calloused fingers softly trace against my cheek, making me smile without opening my eyes as I hum in satisfaction.

"Does that feel nice?"Ly's smooth voice asks in my ear.

"Mmmmm," I mumble incoherently, as my lips stretch wider.

"How about this?"He questions, moments before his lips brush against the side of my neck, making me shiver as my toes curl. "And this?" He rasps, moving his lips an inch lower.

"Yes," I gasp, trying to stay in the moment, but questions are battering my mind. "Ly what are we doing?"I ask, unable to stop myself, even when he brushes a feather soft kiss to my collar bone.

"Anything you want, my princess, " He growls, his words vibrating against the top of my breast, through my thin vest.

"Anything?" I moan, as he pulls my top down slowly, his nails scraping against my sensitive skin, leaving a trail of distracting fire in their wake. "What am I?" I ask, trying not to get distracted.

"You're powerful and amazing," he answers confidently, before his lips close over my taut nipple.

"But where am I from?" I gasp, changing direction as his tongue flicks out.

"Far from here my princess," he murmurs, before sucking my nipple into his mouth, making my mind go blank as a long moan escapes my throat. "I can take you back," he mumbles against my fevered skin. "I can take you far away from here."

"How?" Dina's quiet growl has my eyes wanting to open, "they're both too powerful to be trained together with no protections." She sounds desperate as I force my eyes to stay closed, and my breathing to remain steady.

"I know that," Jace growls back just as frustrated, "but they have to learn." He finishes.

"It will be like lighting a beacon, the moment we let either of them use their magic, have you considered that you moron?"

"I have, but what other option do we have?" He fires back just as fast, "they need their powers active and reliable, if either of them are to survive what's hunting them." I've never heard Jace's voice sound so bleak and dark. I kinda feel bad for eavesdropping on their conversation, but I'm also sure that if me and Charleene were awake they wouldn't be discussing this.

"I know," Dina sighs, "we'll have to keep moving, be careful and vigilant." She mumbles as though speaking to herself.

"You can stop secretly listening-in now Ally," Jace's amused tone has me groaning as he busts my attempt to feign sleep. "How much did you hear?"

"Enough," I answered, rubbing the sleep from my eyes. "How long was I out for?"

"Only about an hour," Dina answers from the back seat, as my eyes adjust to the sunlight, and my nose smells something delicious. "Hey no fair you guys ate while I slept?" I accuse making them both burst out laughing.

"We did but don't worry I've got you covered Ally." Jace explains nodding at the floor near my feet, to a brown paper bag with a Mcdonalds logo on the side.

Smiling, I reach down and lift the bag to my lap, letting silence fill the car as I look inside and see the Breakfast wrap box staring up at me. Carefully taking out the wrap and opening it, I slide the two extra hash browns out of their packets before taking a bite out of one and groan in satisfaction as its salty flavour hits my tongue. " Okay, you're forgiven," I mumble to them both as I take a massive bite of the wrap. "So where are we going next?" I ask with my mouthful, gaining me an unimpressed glance from Jace.

"We'll be stopping soon so Jace can have a break from driving," Dina informs me from the backseat.

"Mmmm-hummm," I mutter back, as my mind wonders where we'll be stopping for this break. I look out the window at the other cars passing us in the other lanes of the motorway. "And where will we be stopping?" I ask before shoving more fries in my mouth.

"Kirby Hall, near Northampton," Dina responds quietly, making me glance back to see Charleene's head resting on her shoulder as she sleeps. Her mouth wide open, and I'm pretty sure she's drooling, but Dina either doesn't notice or doesn't care. Smiling, I meet Dina's strange brown and silver eyes as they bore into mine, almost as if she's daring me to say something. When I don't, she softens—well as much as a stone statue can soften anyway—before continuing, "I know someone there who can help hide us for a short time."

"Who?" I ask, not sure about trusting anyone else when I barely trust those within this car.

"An old friend." Dina responds as Charleene stirs next to her.

"Whose an old friend?" She asks around a massive yawn, before pinning Dina with an unflinching stare until her nose twitches, "and is that food I smell?" Without speaking Dina produces another brown Mcdonald's bag from somewhere near her and passes it over. Charleene's squeal of delight makes me smile as she pulls out a cold apple pie, before taking tiny bites, trying not to drop any crumbs.

"Do you really eat dessert before your main?" I scoff, finding it incredibly funny how innocent she is. It's like watching a kid.

"Damn right I do," she happily states, finishing off the last bite before turning back to Dina, "so who's an old friend?" She repeats.

"Gladys Kingsbrook is." Dina's furrowed brow tells me there's more to that statement than she's willing to explain.

"And how will Gladys be able to protect us from mystery vampires and…" my voice trails off as I look over at Jace's tight shoulders.

"She's a witch, not a very powerful one but she's brilliant with protection charms and spells. I want her to train you both in them while we're with her." Dina states looking at both me and Charleene.

"Oookayyy," I mutter back, not liking the idea of this Gladys knowing even more about me. But it would be awesome to learn how to be more helpful.

"Do you really think she'll be able to teach me?" Charleene asks timidly, whilst she nervously picks apart the egg mcmuffin in her lap to pieces.

"Eat." Dina states sternly, and waits for Charleene to put some of it in her mouth before continuing. "Yes, she should babe. It's Her I'm not sure she'll be able to teach," Dina says nodding in my direction.

"Why not?" I question.

"Because your magic is completely different to Charleene's."

"It's ok Ally, I can teach you when we're at a safe place," Jace confidently mentions, speaking for the first time in a while.

"Ok," I grumble, before looking back out the window.

"How long's it gunna take to get us to this Gladys person?" Charleene asks to the car in general.

"About another hour or so." Jace and Dina say at the same time.

This revelation has me and Charleene groaning, I don't know about anyone else but my arse is already feeling pretty numb at this point. Letting out a small sigh, my gaze returns to the cars passing beside us. Can I stand another hour inside this already musty smelling car? Who knows! But, it's not like we have any other option I remind myself, leaning forward and pressing play on the radio. As some random pop song fills the car I let myself zone out, wondering what the hell has happened to Lilah for the millionth time.

My mind conjures different images, each one more horrifying than the last, as I think about the state of our cottage. Counting how many days have already passed since Lilah vanished. "Ally," Jace's voice penetrates my spiraling dark thoughts, making me jump in my seat, and bringing me back to the here and now. Charleene and Dina are mumbling in the back while Jace's concerned eyes search mine, "what are you thinking about?" He asks softly as his finger captures a stray tear before it can fall down my cheek.

"Lilah," I whisper back, afraid that if I speak her name any louder something even worse may happen to her.

"She's tough Ally, she'll be ok." I know he's trying to reassure both of us but I'm not so sure she will be. Instead of voicing this, I just nod and lean my head against my headrest as I glance at the small clock. The bright numbers 7:45 shine cheerfully back at me. *So early,* I think to myself, as my numb bum makes itself known, causing me to shift in my seat.

Half an hour later we're driving slowly down a long and winding country lane, surrounded by well tended fields as far as the eye can see, "Where's all the traffic?" I ask, just before I feel the same tug inside my body as I did when we entered and left Hampstead. "Is it protected?" I mutter receiving a curious glance from Jace.

"Yes, its reality is protected like in Hampsted Alyssa, it's how you'll both stay hidden from our pursuers." Dina answers, also glancing my way with a curious expression.

"So what the general public see isn't what we'll see, right?" Charleene questions, drawing my attention to her, before I can ask about Dina's funny look.

"Correct," Dina answers.

"Oh thank God, because I was thinking how can a person live in a bunch of ruins in England of all places."

"Wait, this place is a ruin?" I really need to start getting out of my head and googling places before I'm always left feeling surprised.

"Yeah," Charleene answers, passing me over her smart phone so I can flick through the pictures she's already looked at.

One of the pictures shows the hall from above and its impressive, rectangular building around the central courtyard, with manicured gardens, in the shade of tall trees and around it is nothing but countryside. "Impressive," I state handing back her phone, "and your friend Gladys owns all of this?"

"Technically the national trust owns it, Gladys rents Kirby Hall out to them and receives a cut of the profits."

Turning a corner, my mouth drops open at the view before me; a tree lined lane takes us right up to the back of the enormous pale stoned building. I'm still staring as Jace parks us next to a small black Citroen C1, in the small, otherwise empty parking area and gets out, coming to my side of the car as I slowly open my door.

"Is everyone you know rich as hell?" Charleene asks breathlessly, pushing herself out of the car and stretching in relief.

"Not everyone," Dina responds distractedly, just before I hear running footsteps approaching us from the building. Moments later, a tiny woman emerges from the door.

"Adrina!!" She yells excitedly in a high pitched voice that hurts my ears, "what are you doing here?"

"Gladys," Dina greets her warmly, before being dragged into a bear hug from the tiny lady, "We needed a safe place to rest for an hour or two." She answers as Gladys steps back before turning and taking us all in.

"And who are your friends Drina?" She asks with a confused frown.

"That's Alyssa and Jace," She says nodding her head at us, "and this is Charleene." She states going to her side and linking their hands together, making Gladys' frown deepen.

"Well you better all come in, I've got breakfast, come on," she demands before walking back to the small wooden door and holding it open for us.

Glancing once at Jace with a raised eyebrow before following Dina, Charleene and Gladys inside, I survey my surroundings. "Wow," I mutter under my breath as we leave the bright sunshine behind and are instantly transported back in time.

"Yep, it's a shame that not everyone gets to see Kirby Hall in all its splendor but..." Gladys responds to whatever Charleene just said before letting her voice trail off.

"It's beautiful" she says in return, making my eyes return to the hall we're currently walking down.

"Elizabethan elegance in all its finest," Gladys responds proudly, as we file into the kitchen that's a mashup of old and modern appliances. A long, black marble worktop flows seamlessly into a built-in electric hob, then to a massive porcelain sink, as a giant fridge/freezer hums away in the corner. A massive wooden table dominates the empty space, with ten grey bar stools placed around it.

Mystified, I perch on one of the stools and keep looking around the kitchen. "How do you live in such a big place?" I wonder out loud.

Gladys' laughter has my head whipping around so fast, I think I've given myself whip-lash. "What?" I ask confused as I glance between them.

"Drina, have you been exaggerating again?" she asks fondly as she pulls four tinfoil wrapped packages from the oven, "I don't live here, Alyssa was it?" Nodding, I wait for her to explain. "I live in a small cottage right on the edge of the grounds." She explains placing a package in front of all of us except Dina.

"So why keep this place secret?" I wonder aloud as I slowly unwrap the tinfoil.

"To protect it over the years."

"From who?" Charleene answers around a mouthful of food.

"Robbers, rich bastards that would want to own it for themselves," she shrugs, "it's been in my family for the last couple hundred years or so and as witches it gave us a big enough place to meet." Gladys' green eyes study Charleene intently before continuing, "but you should be familiar with coven practices hmmm?"

Her question makes Charleene flinch as Dina bristles and protectively wraps an arm around her shoulders before speaking, "Charleene doesn't have a coven Gladys," she gently answers, "it's one of the reasons we came here…"

"No coven?" Gladys gasps, "what did you do?" She questions narrowing her eyes at Charleene. The insinuation in her tone has my blood rising, even as I try to keep my anger under control.

"She did nothing wrong," I boldly state even though I know nothing about the girl's history, "why would you even jump to that conclusion?" I demand, feeling my power bloom inside me, as my anger on Charleene's behalf rises higher, drawing Gladys' attention.

"Because either her coven is dead or they banished her," she says flatly pointing at Charleene, "witches protect our own, so which is it youngling?"

"I...I...I don't know?" Charleene stutters as tears fill her eyes.

"Adrina! What have you dragged me into this time, old friend?" Gladys' tone is furious as she studies me and Jace closer, and I feel flames lick the back of my clenched fists, "why are you traveling with ancient ones and protecting an unknown witch?"

"It's a long story Gladys," Dina says slamming her hand down on the ancient table and making it shake, "Charleene is part of the Nicnevin coven," she pauses and lets that tidbit sink in, before pointing at me and Jace, "and as to those two they shouldn't even be here! But they are, so I've been tasked with making sure they leave. And hopefully soon."

"The Nicnevin Coven?" Gladys questions, "Drina they haven't been seen or heard from in what twenty plus years! And you're right about those two, their kind do not belong here."

Charleene's gasp has all of us looking at her, as tears fill her eyes, "babe what's wrong?" Drina questions softly.

"I'm twenty Dina," Charleene whispers and I connect the dots before Dina does.

"Charleene just because they've not been seen in your lifetime does not mean they are gone." I state with conviction.

"Then where are they? And why was I adopted as a small child?" Charleene asks in an unsteady voice, "why did they abandon me if they're alive?"

"I don't know babe, but she's right," Dina confirms, nodding in my direction but her eyes not leaving Charleene's, "the high council would not have sent us searching for them if they were dead, please don't cry babe."

"Bloody Hecate and all her spirits!" Gladys suddenly exclaims, making all of us jump, "Adrina have you finally..."

"Shhhh!" Drina interrupts before Gladys can finish her sentence, pinning her with a death glare that scares the shit out of me, but only makes Gladys laugh harder and shake her head.

"You're definitely in a heap of trouble Drina," she laughs,

before turning to the rest of us, "eat up you can all tell me just what the hell is going on while we eat I'm starving."

Lifting the polystyrene lid I gasp in surprise at the bacon butty sitting inside, smiling, I grab the sandwich and begin demolishing it as Dina explains everything she knows and the reason we're here.

"Ok then." Gladys says once everyone's boxes are empty, "lets see what I'm working with," she states matter of factly, as if this sort of thing happens to her daily. Hell, it might well happen to her daily, she's certainly not that bothered by Dina randomly dropping by as we follow her out into the grounds. She leads us away from the manor house. Far away I notice, glancing anxiously behind us as it shrinks into the distance.

"Erm where are we going," I whisper to Jace, trying not to show my sudden unease.

"Calm yourself Forgotten, we don't need you to explode before we're hidden again," Gladys tosses back at me as she continues on to a small cottage enclosed by trees.

A soft warm hand suddenly wraps around mine, startling me as Charleene whispers, "I'm scared too," making me glance across at her and smile, as we step over fallen branches and dodge piles of dirt.

Gladys passes through a small gap in the hedge, then Dina disappears, soon followed by Jace, as Charleene and I trade nervous glances. Neither of us are excited to be stepping into the unknown again. Taking a big gulp of air, I squeeze Charleene's hand once, before yanking her after me into a massive garden.

"Right let me look at you both properly, stand here," She motions for me to move a few steps to my right, "and you here Charleene," Gladys says pointing to a space about ten steps to my left.

"What do you mean look at us properly?" Charleene asks timidly, watching Gladys closely.

"I'm going to try and see what led you both here and try to determine the magic waking inside each of you."

Clenching my hands into balls, I try not to be terrified by her words, "you want to look into our pasts?" I ask quietly.

"Yes Forgotten, I do. You are clearly here for a purpose, and I believe that Charleene here is as much a part of your journey as you are of hers."

"Why are you calling me that? I have a name you know," I snark back at her, mystified by her words.

"Because you are of the Forgotten race, who left so long ago that you are now just a half remembered myth. Humans think you are a mystical race, but we, the supernatural, we know your kind abandoned us many moons ago. So yes, you have a name. But- you are also Forgotten to Witches."

"Hhmmm, well do you mind using my name?" I ask sharply, and I know I'm being rude but I'm getting so sick of everyone knowing more about me than I do.

"Very well Ally, I'll start with Charleene and then try and see you," she says nodding to me. "Both you ladies be seated. And you two," Gladys barely glances at Dina and Jace, "make yourself scarce."

"I'll be fine Jace," I mutter, putting him a little bit at ease before Dina drags him from the garden, leaving me and Charleene alone with a witch we don't know.

"Right Charleene, please relax this shouldn't hurt, we are sisters in a fashion. I mean you no harm." Gladys' voice is calm and motherly as she instructs Charleene on what to do next, "Close your eyes and find one thought or place that makes you feel safe." Gladys waits a few seconds as Charleene's worried brow smoothes out, and a small smile graces her lips. "Have you got it?" She asks, and Charleene nods. "Good now sink into that feeling, let the peace flow through you." Gladys lets her own eyes fall shut and I watch as the purest white glow slowly pulses around her body, looking over to Charleene I can see the same glow surrounding her as her breathing steadies.

After what feels like hours, Gladys' eyes snap open. But, instead of seeing her normal eye colour they look cloudy. Her lips begin whispering incoherently, until words finally burst forth "From the ancient lines will come two children, both hunted, betrayed, and loved. Entwined with forces dark and light, of one world but open to many. One will be our salvation, the other our destruction. As ancients return, battles will wage. For gates long shut will be opened, and bridges long burned will be repaired." Gladys' voice rings hauntingly in the silence of the garden, her words making me shiver before her eyes snap open and she grabs her head.

Jumping towards her, I'm almost touching her when Charleene's voice stops me dead, "don't touch her!" She screams, making me grab my hand back as though I'd been burned.

"What's wrong with her?" I ask, concerned as Charleene just sits and watches.

"She'll be fine, but if you startle her she may lash out, she's still inside the connection."

"Cryptic much?" I mutter under my breath as my eyes return to Gladys as she hunches forward.

"I can feel her still looking inside, trying to find what's hidden." Charleene explains with a confused look on her face.

"And what's hidden inside of you exactly?"

"I have no idea?" Charleene laughs nervously as the white glow begins to dim around them both.

"And neither do I." Gladys suddenly announces, making both of us jump, "Someone locked you up tight as a baby."

"Why?"

"To protect you, to protect us? Only they who placed the lock on you will know," she looks concerned at Charleene, before turning to me, "what happened while we were connected?" She asks in a no nonsense voice and a steely look, so I repeat everything that happened from the moment she closed her eyes.

"You're a child of the prophecy Charleene, that is why someone went to great lengths to hide you."

"But why? And which one am I?" Charleene's voice grows higher and higher as she panics.

"Only time will tell, but I do know that children suspected of being connected to that prophecy have been killed for centuries by their own covens."

"I don't want to destroy anything, I couldn't, I wouldn't…."

"Ssshhh child, what many fear is that the child will not have much choice in what they do. Many coven leaders have passed that fear onto their own children, generation after generation. You have to remember, no-one likes the unknown."

"Plus you might not even be one of these children," I interject and bring both of their focuses to me.

"Maybe not," Gladys says, but from her concerned look I know she doesn't believe me, "your turn Forg…Ally." She swiftly says, motioning me back to my designated spot.

Sceptically, I move back and sit down, following the same instructions she gave Charleene. I tried to think back to any time when I'd actually felt safe. Letting my mind wander, through memories both real and imagined until one grabs me. I'm being held, strong arms enclose me from behind. I can't see the person's face but I know they'll protect me, keep me safe.

"Have you got it?" Gladys' voice interrupts the feeling briefly. Without opening my eyes I nod, and anchor myself in this person's arms as the real world drifts away.

"Found you," his voice croons into my ear, making me shiver, "you can't hide from me Princess."

"Alysium!" A women shouts, interrupting his seductive voice. She sounds frantic and distant, as though she's shouting over a great distance. "Run my child, Run!" She shouts, and her fear worms through my sense of calm.

"Mother?" I question, as I feel pressure being applied gently to the walls around my mind.

"Fight Alysium!" She demands, her command ringing in my head as terror floods me. "Push him away!" Is the last thing I hear before my power begins to build, feeding on the terror I now feel, and before I can do anything I explode.

Chapter Seventeen

Alyssa.

"Ally, where are you?" His voice asks from the dark.

"Ly?" I question as my eyes search, needing to see anything other than the dark.

"Where are you? I can't find you?" He questions again, as I stumble forward a step.

"I'm right here, please find me." I gasp as panic creeps in, making my head whip side to side. "Lysais!" I scream, needing to feel his arms around me, needing anyone to banish the darkness.

"Tell me where, my love?" Does his voice sound further away? Yes? No? I don't know.

"Find me!" I scream, just as something builds inside me, feeding from my need for light. Squeezing my eyes shut, I let it blast out of me and for a brief second I see his face before my light blinds me.

"Yes Alysium, let it out." He growls at me.

"What exactly is she?" Dina's voice shrieks through my foggy mind as I float in darkness. "Jacin, what type of ancient one is she?"

"It doesn't matter," He growls back.

"It most definitely does, she's a ticking time bomb. None of us understand what triggers her, maybe if we knew what race she belongs to, it might help."

"Ally? Ally? Please wake up...you have to wake up." His voice sounds so broken that I force my eyes open, meeting his hazel ones that shine with unshed tears.

"What happened?" I ask quietly.

"Maybe you could tell us?" Gladys probes gently, drawing my attention to where she and Dina are bending over Charleene.

"Oh My God what did I do? Is she alright?" I ask my questions running into each other as I try to sit up, and the world spins so fast I let myself flop back down.

"I was using the same spell I used on Charleene, just a simple searching spell meant to show me your past. But as I pushed past your shields—impressive by the way—you screamed no, and the next thing I know I can feel your power rising inside. I barely managed to get a shield up in time, and unfortunately I wasn't quick enough to protect Charleene." Gladys explains, as I cover my eyes to hide my tears.

"Is she..." I can't even utter the word, but everyone knows what I'm asking.

"No. She's not waking up, but she's also not dead Ally." Jace explains gently, while helping me to slowly sit up.

"What do you mean not waking up, what did I do this time?"

"If my suspicions are correct, then I think you lashed out using a more concentrated form of the element we call spirit. When I tried pushing past your barriers, it made you feel unsafe or threatened, so you used the same element to attack who your mind perceived as an intruder. But you're so strong, much stronger than I've ever seen, I think you caught Charleene and somehow locked her inside her own spirit."

"WHAT!" I scream panicking for Charleene, "How? How do I fix this?"

"You can't," Gladys states, giving me a curious look.

"What do you mean I can't?" I ask as Dina angrily shouts, "she bloody well will fix her!"

"The only person that can fix Charleene now is herself," Gladys patiently explains to all of us, "once a person is trapped within their own spirit they must find their own way back, I can protect her body. But she won't have long."

"How long?" Dina growls bending over Charleene protectively.

"Five days, maybe six?"

"And what happens if she's not back by then?" Dina quietly asks what we're all thinking.

"Then she'll move on from this life and return to the Mother of us all." Gladys explains.

"No, no, no, I can't lose her Gladys, I can't not now." Dina gasps out, meeting Gladys eyes.

"I know an old friend who might know something more. But she is strong, and I don't think her journey ends here. Take heart in that Drina, your amour is a fighter."

Nodding, Dina spears me with a murderous glare. "No more magic from you!" she demands.

"It's not like I can help it," I grumble under my breath, but of course she hears it with her damn vampire hearing.

"I don't care, learn to control it." She snaps at me, before lifting Charleene and heading back towards the manor and our car.

"Bitch." I snap before stamping after them.

"She's not wrong Ally, you need to learn how to control these outbursts," Jace's reasonable tone almost pitches my anger over the edge, but the concern on his face stops me short.

"Maybe I would if I knew more!" I snap before I can stop myself, "I heard my mother's voice Jace, just before it happened." I whisper, waiting for him to call me crazy.

"What? You heard Lilah? How?"

"No, not Lilah. I heard my birth mother's voice Jace. At least, I think it was her, it's hard to explain." I know my explanation is confusing, hell I'm confused! Between my damn dreams, these explosions of power and all the unexplainable things that keep happening, I'm certain, "I've gone insane."

"You're not insane, Ally," Jace tells me, making me realise I'd spoken that thought aloud. "Tell me what happened before?"

His reasonable tone has my mouth opening to tell him, until I glance over at him, missing the root as it snags my foot. Pain bursts up my leg, my ankle twists and gravity grips me, pulling me down as I lose my damn balance. Jace, moving faster than I've ever seen, has my arm trapped in a vice-like grip—before I can even let out a scream—keeping me from smashing face first into the ground, "what's happening to me?" I plead, desperately needing to know the answer. I watch as his face shuts down. "Oh that's right you won't tell me." I scoff, watching as pain flashes in his brown eyes. "Well you can't demand my secrets if you're unwilling to share your own Jace," I continued, shutting him out, anger making my heart harder as Jace flinched away from me.

"I can't explain, I wish I could tell you everything, you don't know how much I wish I could Ally," he muttered at me, but I was sick of hearing him make excuses.

"But you can't." I finish for him, pinning him in place with a death glare, "you have all the answers but can't share them. When did you become so secretive Jace? We used to tell each other everything for as long as I can remember we never hid anything."

"Ally, please?"

"No, just shut up, damn it." I shout, letting my frustration free, "if this was you I'd still tell you, no matter if it hurts because not knowing is killing me. And not being able to trust you makes it ten times worse." I finish quietly, letting him know just how pissed I am, before storming ahead.

"Everything will make sense again, we just need to find Lilah. She'll know what to do," he says to my back in a small voice. Ignoring him, I pick up the pace until I can see Dina's back.

"So what do we do now?" Jace asks her, breaking our tense silence, as we catch up with her, walking side by side to the house.

"The same as before we keep going to Scotland and hope she wakes up." Dina answers coldly, meeting my gaze with such a cold look I swear the temperature actually dropped a few degrees.

"We could stay here for a few days," I suggest trying to be helpful.

"No we need to keep you both moving," She and Jace say in unison as I glance between them. *Since when did they become mind readers?* I think sarcastically.

"Why?"

"Ally please, just trust us." Jace pleads as we walk towards a sitting room.

"Are you going to tell me the truth?" I ask back, waiting for his answer. When one doesn't come, I look away. "Well then, you answered your own question. No. I can't trust you." I say, already feeling bad for pushing him away. "What are we running from? And don't say Lysias, he's the only one that seems willing to tell me the truth." I spit at him.

"I don't know why you ever trusted that piece of..." Jace growls, letting his own anger get the best of him, before snapping his mouth shut.

"What is that supposed to mean?" I scream, spinning around to glare at him.

I'm still staring daggers at him, when Dina's voice lashes out at us both like a whip in the silent room. "Will you two stop behaving like children, you're grown adults for god's sake." Meeting her gaze, I'm about to give the high and mighty vampire a piece of my mind when I look down at Charleene's pale face, and all my anger dries up. She's ghastly pale against the deep blue of the sofa cushions, but her eyes move rapidly under her eyelids, almost as if she's dreaming.

"Sorry," I mumble, feeling like a dick as she gently clears a few strands of dirty blonde hair from Charleene's brow. We have bigger things to worry about than mine and Jace's crap. "Where are we going?" I ask gently, my gaze returning to Charleene.

"I know someone who might be able to help Charleene, I mean it's a long shot but he might be able to do something." Gladys announces as she comes into the room, carrying a tray of hot drinks.

"Who?" Dina snarls her eyes never once leaving Charleene's face.

"Donovan. I think he was up near Doncaster, last I checked in with him." She answers politely, ignoring Dina's tone completely, as my hands wrap around the warm cup she passes me. Lavender and rose fill my nose alongside something else I can't name, as I instinctively sniff at the steam. "It will keep you calm" Gladys explains before handing a black mug to Dina. "Donovan is a witch specifically trained in the spirit element. If anyone can help Charleene, other than her own coven of course, it's him."

"Where?" Dina snaps, before taking a sip of what I'm guessing is blood. Where the heck did Gladys get blood from? I wonder briefly, before sighing and taking a burning sip of my own drink.

"He took over Cusworth Hall a few years back, I think he's still there. I'll give him a call while you all finish your drinks." Gladys gives a small smile to Jace and I before leaving the room again.

Blowing on my herbal tea I wander around the room, looking at the paintings and knick-knacks in detail as we wait. I don't think Dina wants me to utter a word, and I definitely don't want to talk to Jace right now. So, carefully sipping the amazing Lavender infused water, I find myself staring at a delicate blue and white tea-pot.

Gladys' voice has me jumping as it comes from right behind me, "it's Victorian, so don't break it."

"Oh right," I mutter, not really caring about how old it is. "Is it time to go?" I ask dreading getting back into the car with those two.

"It is. I've already spoken to Drina and Jace, but I think you needed more time," it's only then that I notice we're alone. "Do not tell Donovan what you are, he'll suspect sure enough, but don't confirm it. Not everyone should know your kind are among us again."

"I don't even know what my kind is and I thought you said we could trust this Donovan?.."

"You're the Ancient ones, the ones that we witches are descended from. You my Dear are Fae. And if I'm correct, you're a gatekeeper." She all but whispers as I stare at her in disbelief and confusion.

"What's a gatekeeper?" I ask just as quietly, imitating her tone even though we're alone.

"I'm going to tell you a story, one that isn't spoken of anymore. When I was but a small girl my mother would tell me cautionary tales of the Gatekeeping Fae, meant to keep little witches in line; if you're naughty the Gatekeeper Fae will take you, don't stray too far Gladys or the Gatekeeper Fae will steal you away. That sort of thing. But one night, when I got older, I asked her who they were."

"And who were they?" I breathe out quietly, when she doesn't continue.

"My mother wouldn't say, but as I grew up I couldn't get her tales out of my head so I began researching them. I hunted down the legends that mentioned them. The Gatekeepers were one of the first lines of Fae. They had great elemental powers, but their most coveted power was the ability to forge gateways between worlds. They lived on every world, keeping peaceful order between species for centuries. But then- I couldn't find out exactly what happened, but there are vague mentions that one went crazy, and began wanting to rule all the worlds. In the end a hunt ensued, and every gatekeeper and their children were hunted down and killed."

"What?" I gasp, astonished by their brutal end.

"You are strong Alyssa, even for Fae-kind," Gladys' states confidently, as her soft hands grip mine hard, "and you're here in our world for a reason. What if some of those gatekeepers escaped their fate and fled?" She questions.

"And you think what? That I'm some descendant of this ancient line?" I laugh incredulously at even thinking I might have something so rare and dangerous.

"Only time will tell, but I fear if you do, you will also be hunted." Gladys sadly explains.

"By whom?" I ask wrapped up in her strange tale.

"By everyone, my Dear."

"Why are you telling me this?"

"Because Hecate tells me you need to know." She answers with a mischievous grin.

"Well thank you and all, but I think I should get going." I mutter, before walking briskly to the door.

"Be well ancient one, but be careful. The devil wears many masks," she utters, just as I step into the hall, making me shiver. *Strange woman*, I think glancing back once to see her watching me, before I all but run from the house.

"There you are."Jace calls over from the car as I burst out into the sunshine of another glorious autumn day. "Get in, Dina's impatient, she wants to get to this Donovan guy as fast as we can." He explains as I run towards the car, "what did Gladys want you for anyway?" Jace asks curiously as I climb into the front seat.

"Nothing, just some mumbo jumbo story about the Fae and Gatekeepers" I mutter distractedly.

"Gatekeepers?" Jace's tone has me almost snapping my neck to look over at him, "what did she say Ally?"

"What does it matter to you? If she wanted you to know she'd have told you herself." I explain before sticking my tongue out and staring out my window ignoring him as he tries to get me to talk.

"Ally, please talk to me?" Jace pleads.

"Just leave it alone Jace." I snap back, closing my eyes and ignoring everyone as the car starts moving.

"We're here," Lys' voice whispers in my ear, as he removes his hand from my eyes.

"And where is here?" I giggle and try to glance around at him, but can't twist my neck enough.

"You tell me princess?" He rasps before placing a kiss on my neck, "where are you?" His deep voice touches me in places that it shouldn't be able to reach, making me shiver as we're suspended wherever we are.

"It's a secret Ly, I'm not allowed to tell." I whisper in a breathy moan as his lips travel up and down my neck beneath my ear.

"You can tell me all your secrets princess, you already know that," he whispers back.

"And what secrets do I have?" I find myself unable to resist playing along.

"Hmmmmm," he rumbles against my skin, "you're playing hide and seek my love."

Shivering, and wanting him to kiss me even lower, I twist in his arms and stare into his beautiful blue ones, "I'm right here, I'm not hiding." I smirk before gently reaching up to kiss his lips.

Just before my lips reach his, he steps away letting frigid air swirl between us, "where are you princess?" He asks again, but his voice has changed, he sounds angry and his fingers are digging into my arms painfully.

"Who are you?" I ask confused, the Lysias of my dreams has never hurt me but he is now.

"It's me, my love." He snaps clearly frustrated with me, "where are you Alysium?" He snarls as his fingertips draw blood.

"Let me go," I sob, "you're hurting me!" Frightened, I try to break free but his grip only tightens.

"You can run Princess, but can't hide from me!" Ly threatens as I'm shaken awake.

"Ally wake up!" Jace screams, shaking me awake.

"W...Where am I?" I ask, glancing around the car, still groggy from the dream or whatever the hell that was.

"We're almost at Cusworth Hall," he states without taking his eyes off the road, "you were having a nightmare."

"Yeah. I'm awake now so it's all good." I snap, brushing off his arm and stretching in my seat.

"Ally?"

"What?" I snap, knowing I should be the bigger person; rise above, forgive him and all that, but I can't. Rubbing my upper arms, I flinch as pain blooms under my fingers, flicking my eyes to Jace. I see that he knows something's wrong with me, but it had been a dream, hadn't it?

"I'm worried about you Ally," he pauses, glancing back at Dina and Charleene in the backseat before continuing, "you're acting strange. Well, more strange than normal," he jokes "what's going on in that head?"

"Nothing," I spit. Not wanting him to know about my dream. One because they're just dreams, I mean they have to be and two, I'm afraid he'd find a way to stop them. He isn't the most rational when Lysais is mentioned. I watch as he opens his mouth before snapping it closed again and returning his gaze to the road before us.

"Well aren't you two at odds," Dina pipes up from the back

making me jump. I think it's the first time she's spoken since we got in the car.

"So what or Who is waiting for us at Cusworth Hall?" I ask, trying to distract myself from the pain on my arms and my very strange dreams. Why has Ly changed, what's made him so angry at me? Shrugging off my thoughts, I focus back on Dina's voice as she explains more about the mage waiting for us.

"Donavon from an old line of witches, ones gifted with sight and spirit," Dina explains in a bored tone. "Gladys says he'll be expecting us," Dina explains, her eyes never leaving Charleene's face. If I didn't know any better, I would have thought she was just sleeping. "Take this next left."

Returning my eyes to the road, I watch as Jace smoothly takes the turn and we drive up another secluded private road. "Do all witches have big private homes?" I ask, utterly bewildered with how much money all these witch friends of Dina's seem to have.

"They're custodians, they don't own the houses, just keep them safe." Dina patiently explains, speaking as though she's talking to a toddler.

"Keep them hidden from humans, you mean?" I say like a smart-ass, wanting to get a rise out of her. *Do not prod the angry vampire!* My inner voice snaps at me, amused.

"Safe, hidden, what's the difference, if humans knew of the artifacts inside these buildings, all they'd do is pilfer them. There are enough rich people, ruling over the poor in this world without a care, just waiting to make themselves even richer."

Her reasoning was sound so I don't argue against it, letting the subject drop as silence filled the car. Sunlight briefly illuminates a private property sign in bold black writing, before the road bends to the right, and a very large stately home appears before us. It rises higher the closer we get, three wings stretch out in a blocky 'u' shape, as I find myself speechless at its beauty.

"Not what you were expecting?" Dina asks as we pull up before the huge entrance door.

"Not at all," I breathe out as I try taking it all in at once. "What happened to the barrier?" I asked innocently, wondering why I hadn't felt its borders.

"It's a protected building, not hidden," Dina states. "The museum is open to anyone wanting to visit it," she continued, her voice softening as she lifted Charleene from the back of our car.

"You could have just said that earlier, you know?" Jace admonishes her softly, leaving me alone. Scrambling to join them I almost fall out of the car, as my feet get tangled with each other. I'm just within touching distance of Jace, when a middle aged man with thinning blond hair greets Dina warmly, with a thin smile, at the door. He apprises Charleene before turning and briskly leading us inside Cusworth Hall.

As Dina explains why we're here, I let myself take in the house. There's history everywhere, glass cases filled with a variety of objects, paintings showing glimpses of different times hang on the walls, with the odd statue here and there. My eyes can't keep still, bouncing from one thing to another, as I try taking in all the history that's been collected and put on show here. Following Jace's broad back, I imagine myself as an elegant lady of old. A step creaks under my foot, dragging me out of my imaginings as we climb a set of wooden stairs to the floor above. Halfway down the next hallway I gasp, as barrier magic brushes against my skin, startling me and drawing Donovan's cool blue stare briefly, before he gestures Dina at a doorway.

Donovan barely glances my way as he shows me and Jace to a different room on the same floor, "I'll see you both once I've seen the Vampire's witch." Donovan explains softly, before turning and leaving me alone with Jace.

"Ally, please..."

God he's like a broken record. "Just. Don't!" I interrupt forcefully, not wanting to hear whatever excuse he's come up with this time to explain his lack of trust in me. He wants to keep secrets? Fine, two can play at that game. "I'm tired." I utter flinging myself down on the soft four-poster bed that takes up nearly the whole room, it even has fucking curtains. Damn it's like I'm suddenly living in a Jane Austin novel, I can picture any one of her characters pacing this very room. Smiling, I let myself drift off, ignoring Jace as he shuffles around.

"Where are you my Princess?" Ly's smooth voice sends shivers down my spine even in my dreams.

"I'm with you," I answer back, hoping that he really was here and not back in his father's hell.

"No you're not, but I want to be with you my love." He growls, making another shiver go through me.

"I'm right here," I repeat, smiling coyly as I roll towards his voice and open my eyes.

"Tell me where?" Ly growls shifting closer to me, as his blue eyes bore into mine, "princess where are they hiding you?" He asks, running a finger up and down my arm, distracting me from all the questions in my head. "They're keeping us apart my love," he whispers against my ear.

"Who are?" I question, not understanding when we're right here together.

"The halfling and your new friends, princess, let me in," he whispers seductively, "let me take you away."

"Hmmmm," I mumble, as his tongue traces the shell of my ear.

"Tell me where you are Princess?" he repeats, it's like his mantra as my heart beats double time, and goosebumps erupt along my skin.

"Yes," I whisper, barely concealing the moan that rises in my throat as his hand softly trails over my suddenly bare stomach.

"Tell me..." He croons into my ear.

"I'm..."

"Ally!" Jacin's panicked voice drags me from my dream, his shaking ripping me away from Ly.

"Wake her up," a new voice demands close by. "She must wake up, if you wish to remain hidden," he explains to Jace as if I'm not here.

"I can hear you, ya know," I mutter, not expecting either of them to listen to me.

"Ally, do you know where you are?" Donovan's quiet voice has my eyes meeting his steely blue ones, and the frown creasing his brow.

"I'm at Cusworth Hall?" I replied confused as to why he'd ask me that. It's not like I hit my head or anything, "I'm not crazy you know." I deadpan staring into his eyes.

"No one said you were Ally." Donovan answers as his lips twitch up at the sides, making him look a tiny bit less stern. "Dream-walking is a dangerous thing Ally, and sometimes the mind does not always come back." Donovan patiently explains.

"Dream-walking? What the hell is dream-walking?" I ask not really knowing if I want to find out.

"When sleeping, a person's mind is vulnerable. While your body stays still in the waking world, your mind travels. Now, for instance, in the old texts we are warned about the dream-walkers, beings who can walk inside the dreams of others." I shiver as I think of how my dreams have changed recently. "It can be very dangerous for both the walker, and the person whose dreams are being invaded. I haven't seen dream-walking for a very long time." Donovan glances between me and Jace, a question clear in his eyes.

"Ally, what have you been dreaming of?" Jace asks, concerned as he meets my gaze.

"They're just dreams Jace," I say exasperated, still refusing to let him know who I'm dreaming of.

"Be careful young-one. Your dreams are not always just dreams I fear," Donovan mutters, before leaving me alone with a very angry Jace.

"Ally! Dream walking, what in the hell are you playing with?"

I know he's exasperated with me, but at the same time I can't find it in myself to care. I've had just about enough of his attitude lately, "Jace you're not my keeper, I don't know what's really going on but I do know that." I snap at him, his macho-man bullshit wearing very thin.

"It's him isn't it?" He spits, stepping closer to me, making my temper snap as I shove to my feet.

"I don't know what the hell is between you two, but he's done nothing to me!" I screech, jabbing him with my finger. "In all of my dreams, and all the times we've met, he's done nothing but protect me and tell me the truth, so until I'm shown otherwise, I trust him." I explain for hopefully the last time, my hard tone leaving no room for argument.

"Ally, you don't know everything," he mutters under his breath, "if you did, you wouldn't say that."

"Your right Jace. I don't know everything and until I do, you would do best to remember that I can and will look after myself." I declare, watching as Jace's anger comes to the forefront, moments before his fist smashes into the wall next to the door and he storms out.

Anger floods through me, simmering beneath my skin, making it feel itchy and tight as I try not to have another magical outburst. My lack of control over this bloody magic was really starting to piss me off. Trying to calm down, I pause when something Donovan said registers in my mind, *'she must wake up if you wish to remain hidden,'* he'd said as I was waking up, how the hell did Donovan know what I'd been dreaming of?

Determined to get answers I fling the door open, flinching as it hits the wall with a bang. Shit, I hope I haven't put another hole in the wall, I think as I begin hunting for Donovan. *Who is this unknown witch that apparently knows far too much about my dreams!*

Chapter Eighteen

Alyssa.

I finally find Donovan in a dim sitting room straight out of a period novel. He barely looks up from his book as I enter. "How's Charleene?" I ask, timidly realising that this was his private place, and I was intruding.

"She is lost," he says slowly, clearly debating how much to tell me. "Her spirit is wandering, and will not return until she finds what she needs," he explains, confusing me even further.

"Can't she be called back?" I ask, hopeful that I might be able to fix my latest mistake.

I wait with baited breath as he ponders my question, "I tried calling her back to her body, but her will is too strong." He pauses watching my reaction, "she will be a powerful witch, when she ascends into her full power." He murmurs, almost as if to himself.

"And you?" I ask, as his brow furrowed in confusion, "you must be pretty powerful yourself for us to have been sent here." I explain, trying to figure out the man sitting before me.

"Hmmmm, both yes and no," Donovan answers with a smirk, making him look ten years younger, and a lot less-detached.

Smiling back, I wonder if he ever answers clearly, "do you always talk in circles?" I half joke as he gestures for me to sit across from him.

"They're clear to me, young-one, but to make it a little easier for you to understand; I'm a powerful seer and spirit user but that is the extent of my powers, which some would say makes me weak." At my bewildered look, he places a bookmark inside his book before continuing, "our powers are drawn from the earth, her goodness radiates through our bodies and we can use its energy like a conduit," I nod, showing that I was keeping up. "Some have an affinity with plants, some with animals, the more powerful of us can draw upon the elements themselves. While most can only draw on one element, there are those who can draw on every element, like your sleeping friend."

"But she doesn't know what magic she has?" I interrupt rudely, as the thought pops into my head.

"She may not. I felt the threads connecting her not only to one element, but to everything around her as well." He explains, "this tells me that she is a powerful witch. But that's not what you came to ask, is it?"He states flatly, as his eyes bore into mine.

"No," I admit sheepishly, dropping his gaze and glancing around the room. "How did you know what I was dreaming about?" I ask, focusing on the overflowing floor to ceiling bookcases behind him.

"When I was searching for Charleene, your mind drew me like a moth to a flame and I stepped into your dream," he pauses at my horrified look as I open my mouth to interrupt, before he hurries on "I didn't mean to but your spirit called to me, forced me to heed its call." Searching his face, I look for anything that will say he's lying but his expression doesn't falter. "And I saw black tendrils, faint shadows trying to wind themselves around your dream self, trying to pull you towards danger."

"How?" I ask, not willing to let myself consider the fact that Jace might have been correct about Ly.

"Whoever controls those shadows means you great harm, Alyssa. I don't know how but I'm certain they will eventually lead you to ruin."

"Right?" I question, still unwilling to believe that Ly would hurt me, "have you seen my future?" Gripping the bottom of my top, I try to stop my hands from shaking as I wait for his answer, as his eyes cloud over.

"Death, loss, love, betrayal, heartbreak all lie in your immediate future Ancient one. I see you broken and alone in the dark. You are the key they seek, a key they cannot wield, or death will come for all." He finishes ominously before his eyes return to their normal colour, and he gives me a strange look I can't decipher.

My head feels like swiss cheese, more damn riddles, "what do you mean?" I ask gently, needing to understand.

"Unfortunately, I can explain no more than that Alyssa, I see only glimpses, snapshots in time. Fate is fickle and doesn't give me everything. Some I see more clearly than others, but your path is wrapped in shadows."

I bristle in the quiet his words leave behind, shuffling in my seat, "why are you helping me Donovan?" I'm confused at why a stranger would help other strangers.

After a couple of minutes Donovan smiles, "that's easy Alyssa. Because you're a good soul."

I smile at his confidence that I'm good, when I don't even really know who I am, or was. Donovan has done nothing in the brief time I've known him to make me not trust him, so I push my luck "can I ask you one more question?" I hesitantly asked, not wanting to piss him off.

"Of course."

"Can you find Lilah?" I ask, noting his look of surprise at my question, before he closes his eyes and his breathing deepens. I'm holding my breath, staring at Donovan's peaceful expression as Dina finds us.

"What's he doing?" She demands nodding her head in Donovan's direction.

"Looking for Lilah I think," I whisper, afraid of making too much noise and disturbing him. Watching him carefully, I notice the slight tightening of his lips before his blue eyes meet mine and he shakes his head. Crestfallen, I look at my feet wondering what to do now. A sharp intake of breath at the door has all of us whipping around, to find Jace watching us all suspiciously.

"Well doesn't this look comfy," he states flatly looking at each of us, before his gaze settles on me.

"Jace, get a grip we were just talking," I state, rolling my eyes so hard I'm sure I almost see the back of my head. I don't know what his problem is this time, "what do you want?" I ask tiredly.

"I want you to be safe Ally, I want for us to find Lilah and for us to go…" He cuts himself off with a snarl as he realises he almost let something else slip again.

Frustrated as he keeps something else from me, I smile apologetically at Donovan before leaving, shouldering my way past Jace in the doorway. "I'm not fragile Jace, I can handle more than you think and I will get answers one way or another." I snap, before finding my way through the house to the grounds. Might as well get some fresh air before we have to start moving again.

The gardens surrounding Cusworth Hall are expansive and beautiful, and I find myself moving further and further away from the house, lost inside my own head. I'm sitting in one of the surrounding fields alone when the grass next to me moves, "Fuck off Jace," I mutter staring at the house in the distance.

"Poor little Princess all lost and alone," a familiar dark voice croons in my ear, making me shiver and jump at the same time.

"You're not here," I whisper, not willing to look at what must be a hallucination.

"Aren't I Princess?" His voice has me shivering both with desire and a little bit of fear, "look at me gorgeous." He states as his finger runs softly up my arm, reminding me again of his grip in my dream.

Slowly, as though caught in a trance, my head turns and I lock eyes with Lysais, shock makes my head slow as I just shake my head, while my hand reaches out to cup his face. "How?" I stutter, when I can finally make my mouth work.

"Tut, tut," he tisks shaking his head, "all that matters is I'm here now." He says with a cheeky grin, as if he's just said the most cheesy thing in the world.

"You shouldn't be here," I murmured, not really wanting him to leave.

"I'll risk everything for you my love," he says, as his fingers graze my cheek, "you need to come with me." I can hear the anger he's trying to hide in his voice, confusing me enough that I'm moving back.

"Why?" I ask, not understanding how he can go from seemingly loving to angry, in the space of a breath.

"I'll tell you everything but you have to come with me, let me take you away?" Shuffling further away, I try to find the answers in his eyes as I notice the cold, calculating way he looks at me.

"Apparently you're dangerous?" I ask gingerly not knowing what to believe anymore.

"Oh, I'm very dangerous Princess. I'm deadly, but you need to come with me." His voice is hard, as if he expects no argument. A warning bell sounds in my head, and I hear Jace's voice in my head warning me about Lysais.

"Then why would I leave with you?" I ask glancing around to see if I can run anywhere.

"Running won't help you foolish Princess," he mocks, "you left their wards, now you're mine." He states darkly, reaching towards me as fear and adrenaline flood my body and my magic answers.

Flinging my hand towards him, I feel the blast of air as it drags past my face and pushes towards Lysais. I hear his vicious snarl as my power pushes him back a step.

"You're no match for me, little girl." He snarls, his lip turning up with it. *He doesn't sound like my Ly*, I think with a shudder.

Panicking, I feel my magic building as a scream gets stuck in my throat, "leave Lysais," I utter through clenched teeth.

"No." He snaps, managing to take a step closer.

"Ally!" Jace's panicked scream momentarily distracts me, almost making me take my eyes of Lysais as he watches me like a hawk. I feel my magic building in response to the fear I suddenly feel, at the angry blazing in his gaze. Unconsciously I let my emotions fuel it, until I feel like I'm burning from the inside out. With a scream I let my tenuous hold on it snap, and close my eyes as I'm encased in a swirling barrier of fire.

"This is not over," I barely hear Lysais snarl over the roaring in my own head, before I feel my head split in two and darkness closes in.

"What?" I ask, giggling like the child I no longer am, "have I got something on my face? I ask, staring into Ly's eyes, trying to read the

thoughts he's hiding behind his damn stoic mask.

"Nothing," he states, with the most boyish smile I've ever seen him wear. It looks silly and goofy, but I absolutely love it.

"I love you." I blurted suddenly, not able to keep it locked away anymore. Butterflies fill my stomach as his smile drops away.

"No! You can't. Ally, I'm no good for you." He growls, angry when I thought he'd be happy. Confused, I again try to read what's going on in his head, as I drag the quilt of flowers further up my bare chest. As Ly begins pulling at his hair in frustration, as dejection begins to run from my heart through my veins, as I realise he obviously doesn't feel as I do.

"Just go!" I whisper before turning my back to him.

"Ally?" His voice almost sets my tears loose but I won't give him that satisfaction, "you don't understand..."

"Just go!" I interrupt, not wanting to hear his excuses about taking my virginity but not wanting me. I feel the bed dip as he moves to the edge of it and brace myself for hearing the door close, but that sound never comes.

"We can't be in love Ally," Scrunching my eyes closed, I shudder at the feel of his calloused fingers running down my neck softly. He's always so patient and gentle with me.

"I don't care," I mumble, losing the battle with my tears and letting them fall, "I've already fallen for you, my heart knew it years ago." I whisper.

My eyes fly open at that revelation, and my heart begins to break for not being able to remember all of my past. "What happened?" I ask, flinching at the pounding inside my head as I speak.

"We need to move," Dina's flat tone pierces my skull, making me whimper, as someone else places a cool cloth on my forehead and I realise I'm laying down, I let my eyes close in relief.

"We will Dina, as soon as they're both stable enough to move." Jace's voice is quiet, barely audible, but at least it doesn't hurt my head.

"What have I done now?" I ask, trying to blink my eyes open

again but my pounding head makes me abandon my attempt.

"You…"

"Not now Adrina." Donovan gently cuts her off, "it appears your dreaming let your whereabouts slip young one, and your enemies have caught up to you." He calmly explains to me as I remember Ly in the field.

"I thought that was another dream," I mutter confused.

"That's the tricky business of dream-walking, what starts as a dream doesn't always remain a dream." Finally I let my eyes open and find his kind, caring ones looking down at me.

"Why does my head feel like I've been on a seven day bar bender?"

"You used your magic again and this time it took its toll," Jace answers from across the room.

"Toll?" I search his eyes as my mind works overtime, telling me that it stole my youth, or my smooth skin. Maybe it made all my hair fall out?

Knowing what my mind was conjuring, Jace's lips quivered in a small smile before putting me out of my misery, "it took some of your energy and it battered against the block in your mind."

"Oh, remind me next time no more magic," I joke rubbing my forehead.

"Next time?" Dina screams, throwing an animalistic glare my way, "there won't be a next time, your magic is dangerous, unpredictable, untamed." She finishes, glaring at Jace as he opens his mouth to disagree before closing it.

It's Donovan's smooth, calm voice that surprises me, "She needs to use her magic, Adrina, how else is she to learn control? It is up to you," he demands pointing in her direction, "to protect them and it's up to you," He turns to Jace next, "to teach them both." His words stun both of them. Even I'm taken aback at the steel behind his words, and the anger in his eyes as he glares at them in turn. "This was done to Alyssa, none of this is her fault so stop blaming her."

Staring at Donovan in shock, it takes me a couple of minutes to respond to his reassuring smile. He's a complete stranger to me but he's got my back. I'm beginning to like him a little more. "Now young one, take this. It will help protect your mind, but it will not last forever." He explains putting a small pendant in my hand and closing my fist around it gently, before shooing everyone else from the room.

"What is it?" I ask quietly, staring at the small milky white stone, clasped in silver.

"It's enchanted moon rock, the best I could do on such short notice, sorry" he answers carefully before explaining how it would only last two weeks if we were lucky, after that Lysais would be able to find me again. "You have to remember to keep it on at all times, he has a link with your dreams, so it won't take him long to find you. Stay safe Young one, I fear you will be needed in the future for all worlds." With his confusing but ominous last statement Donovan left me alone with my thoughts.

Do I really need to block Lysais? Is repeating through my head as I turn the moon rock pendant over in my hand. A soft knock at my door drags my attention away. Breathing deeply I pause as Jace's unique scent filters through the door.

"We need to go," he says gently through the wood.

Chapter Nineteen

Lysais

The new camp was in uproar. Fights had been erupting every couple of hours between the different races; it was a powder keg getting ready to blow as I watched from the sidelines. He'd been reluctant to leave when the bond had tugged in my chest, taking us both by surprise. It should have remained silent until Jacin managed to get her to safety. *So why had it suddenly flared?*

"So fucking close," I taunt, laughing manically in my head as he fumes. I could still smell her intoxicating scent, it was suffocating. I'd been laughing since he'd over stepped in the meadow. Making me push her to come with us had been a massive mistake. Even if she couldn't remember, I'd taught her better than to trust everything at face value. I'd watched closely as her eyes had shuttered, and mistrust of his eagerness made her wary. "She's not fucking stupid." I nudged, wanting his anger to overflow, at least then I might get a few hours of bloody quiet.

"I'll get her, don't you worry, she's in love with you, you bloody idiot. She'll come running when I yank on the bond. Just wait and see." He taunted back. Cutting off any joy I'd just been feeling.

Glancing across the field of monsters waiting to be unleashed, my heart sank as I realised two things: 1. He was right, this bond would have her come running to me, if I wanted it to or not. And 2. He was going to let these monsters lose soon.

Fucking Hell, I snarled at myself wondering if Alyssa was strong enough for what was coming? If we took her home, she'd be tortured, killed, if a worse fate didn't await her there.

My father wanted her for something and his plans never worked out well for anyone but him.

Chapter Twenty

Alyssa.

"Alysium!" Damn it! Can't I get any peace to try and repair my broken heart, I think as Mother's voice calls again, "where are you?" I've managed to evade her for two weeks, but she knows something is wrong. Ly returned to the Shadow realm two weeks ago and I've all but disappeared along with him. Of course she knows something's up.

"What?" I call, giving away my hiding place beneath the willows.

"Don't you what me, Youngling," she admonishes as she pushes the leaves aside, "you have had us worried sick, you barely leave your room, will not let Jacin near you and have been hiding from me and your father! And lets not forget you failed to see Lysias off, and you two are usually joined at the hip. So what is going on with you?"

Opening my eyes, I meet her violet ones that shine with concern for me, "nothing..."

"Do not dare lie to me Alysium," She demands, staring down at me, as my face crumples and I let myself feel the shreds that my heart has become. "Oh Alysium, what has happened?"

"He doesn't want me Mother, I gave him everything and he hates me for it." I sob.

"Who?" she asks kindly, "Jacin?"

"No Ly." I explain feeling a little confused that she'd think I was on about Jacin. Yes we're close, but he's like a brother to me. Ly on the other hand is like the match to my gasoline.

"Ah," she sighs giving me a pitying look, "What have you done Alysium?"

Trying to regain control over my emotions, I take a couple of deep breaths before uttering the words that Ly flung at me before he left, "I've given him a death sentence." I state watching Mother's face carefully, "I created the bond between us and he rejected me." I manage to say before my throat closes up, but I see the horror on her face as my words sink in.

"*Oh Alysium what have you done?*" *I hear the fear in her voice, as it wobbles for the first time I can ever remember.*

"*I fell in love with him Mother, I have been since I first met him.*"

"*Oh my darling girl, you were never supposed to fall in love with him. Anyone but him*"

"*I don't care if everyone hates him, he's not his father.*"

"*Only time will tell that Alysium. Even his father was not always as dark as he is now. But that darkness grew over time, and the madness took over.*" *She trails off, realising what she'd just said as her hands cover her delicate lips.*

"*You know Ly's father? What do you know? Why have you never told me? Why did Ly come to stay with us if his father hates us so much?*" *I shout each question as it comes to mind, wondering what else she has hidden from me over the years.*

"*It's not for you to know Alysium. All you need to know is that this behaviour has to stop.*" *And gone is my caring mother, replaced by the dedicated queen of all.* "*You are my daughter and Heir, this behaviour is highly improper. I expect to see you this evening for the solstice celebrations. And smiling.*"

Jumping to my feet, I level her with my most pitying look before letting my anger reign, "*just because you're as cold as ice, does not mean that I'm heartless too. You're supposed to be my mother, why can't you just act like it for once in my life.*" *I barely register the shock and hurt on her face as I run from her.*

"Ally?" Jace murmured, while shaking me awake, "we're here."

"Here?" I question sleepily, as I glance at the quiet street outside the car. Orange street lights illuminate the tall buildings, each one joined to the next as they continued down the long street, "and where's here?"

"Edinburgh," Dina's clipped answer draws my attention, to her and the silent Charleene in the back seat. One look at Dina's stoney face and I realise she still hasn't woken.

"I thought we had another stop before we'd got here?" Confused, I glanced out the window again. Donovan's had been hours away from Edinburgh.

"We were going to but after Lysais found us at Donovan's, we thought it would be best to come straight here." Jace explains, as a shiver runs down my spine.

"Oh," is the only answer I can give, as I remember the way he'd looked at me. He'd never looked at me so coldly before, in my dreams or in real life. What had I done to make him look at me like that? Why had he looked angry? "So what happens now?" I ask quietly. We've all been speaking quietly around Charleene.

"We'll get settled inside, and then I'm going to meet one of my contacts here." Dina responded before gently picking Charleene's relaxed form from the car.

"How do we know it's safe here?" I asked, looking the street up and down, noticing that not every house had lights on.

"It's one of my spots," Dina answered in a clipped tone, before walking and letting herself into the thin townhouse, as if that statement was all that needed saying on that matter.

Surging out of the car, I opened my mouth to argue when I saw Jace shaking his head. "What?" I asked him exasperated with the lack of answers.

"Not now Ally." He snapped equally exasperated, before grabbing both his own bag and mine from the boot, and following the ladies inside. Shoving down a growl inside my chest, I reluctantly followed.

Inside, my mouth dropped open. The hall was long and thin, ending in a narrow set of stairs that led up to the next floor. The walls held a mixture of photographs and paintings hanging on both walls, each one drew my attention.

They all featured Dina in some way; parties, portraits, you name it, it was there. Everything, except any of Dina as a young girl. As I examined each one closely, I realised Dina's face never changed in all of them; she looked exactly as she does today. If I'd held any doubts of her being immortal before, I certainly wouldn't have any now.

A shuffling of feet had my gaze snapping up to the top of the stairs, and meeting Dina's brown eyes as they glared down at me, making me feel slightly self-conscious at being caught staring at her pictures. "I've put Charleene in my room and there's a spare room at the end of the hall up here, so you'll have to share with Jace." Her tone was as sharp as a whip, shattering the silence of the house.

"Erm, thank you." I muttered.

"She'll need looking after while I'm out," Dina stated.

"Where will you be going?" I asked, not really expecting an answer.

"Jace has my number if she wakes up."

Then, with a blur of movement, I heard the door slam shut as she left. Shaking my head, I made my way up the stairs. Maybe this place would have a bath or at least a shower. Carefully opening the first door on the hallway, I poked my head inside finding a big bedroom with a huge four poster bed. I could just make out Charleene's dirty blonde hair on the pink pillows— huh pink? I would never have pictured Dina with pink sheets. Shaking my head I closed the door softly, leaving Charleene to sleep.

The next door I opened had my mouth dropping open again. There, against the furthest wall, was the biggest bathtub I'd ever seen. The bathroom was gorgeous, with dark marble flooring which contrasted perfectly with the pale grey marble surfaces. Bloody hell, were those gold freaking taps? They certainly looked gold in the faint light I let in from the hall.

Fucking hell yes, I thought to myself, padding over to the deep bath and setting the water warming to the right temperature.

Once the plug was in, I followed the hall down to the final two doors at the end. One opened to reveal another thinner staircase and the other, as promised, was the spare bedroom. It was smaller than Dina's, the double bed only just fitting in. There were no cupboards but, if this was a guest room, I wasn't surprised. What vampire friends would need to store clothes? They probably just bought new ones on their way home. Throwing my bag down on the bed, I grabbed some joggers, a clean t-shirt and my wash bag before returning to her amazing bathroom.

Glancing at the bath, I watched as steam swirled into the air, a smile dancing on my lips as I imagined the warm water covering me. Searching through the tall cupboard behind the door, I found some of the softest towels I'd ever touched, before setting all my clothes on top of the toilet and heading to the massive gilt framed mirror over the sink. Staring at my pale face in the mirror I tried to see any changes, surely with everything in the last twenty-four hours I should have physically changed.

But nope. Nothing, not even an extra wrinkle on my forehead, "you know if you stare hard enough, the mirror might swallow you." Jace's sudden voice had me jumping, and a shriek tore from my throat, as I spun around so fast I almost fell over.

"What the fuck?" I gasped when my lungs would let me, as I frowned at the self-satisfied smirk on his face as it poked through the gap between the door and its frame. "I could have been naked." I growl wiping it from his face.

"If you'd been undressed, the door would have been locked," he stated, trying to dismiss the invasion of privacy.

"And what if I hadn't?"

I watched as he thought for an acceptable answer as my temper began to rise. Drawing in a deep breath, I tried to keep it under control. We couldn't have any more magical mishaps. "I don't know Ally, I honestly didn't think." He said softly, not looking away and I had no answer to spew at him. "Ally I..." He began before cutting himself off again.

"Just spit it out, Jace." I snarled, ready to march over and slam the damn door in his face.

"I just want us back to normal, I miss you,." he whispers as his eyes implored me to accept his olive branch.

"Will you tell me everything?" I asked, wanting us to get back to normal too.

"Ally, you know I can't..."

"Then no, we can't go back Jace," I said sadly, walking to the door and softly closing it, shutting him out as I locked it.

"Ally, please." he implored. I ignored him and went to turn the taps off, "Ally?"

"Just leave me alone Jace," I threw over my shoulder before stripping and sinking into the lusciously warm water with a moan.

The water was almost scalding against my skin and I loved it. Dunking my head beneath the water, so I'm looking up at the distorted ceiling, I allow myself to think about Lilah. The obnoxious sound of her cackle, her kind words of encouragement when life felt too stressful. I didn't realise how much I'd depended on her until she was missing, but it left a giant Lilah shaped hole.

My muscles relax one by one, as the water muffles every sound. The lack of oxygen makes my chest heave, wanting me to break the surface, but I remain submerged until my lungs feel like they're going to burst, and fill my mind with Lilah.

We will find you, we have to! I tell myself, willing my head to believe it.

The house is quiet as I emerge clean, red and surrounded by a cloud of steam. I'd been in the bath for a couple of hours before scrubbing my skin raw. Urggg, I fucking hate traveling. The bedroom door at the end of the hall is closed. Huh. Jace must have got sick of waiting for me to finish up and gone to sleep. I don't poke my head in to check, deciding I'll just sleep on a sofa.

Poking my head in Dina's room, I walk quietly over to the bed and sit beside Charleene.

"Hey you," I start, suddenly not knowing what else to say, but I don't want her to feel alone as I clasp her small hand in mine and force myself to continue. "You're going to have to wake up soon, ya know. You're missing out on all the fun." A snort leaves me at that, what fun?

Driving for hours on end is certainly no fun. Being hunted is definitely not fun, but something in me was screaming; *say anything you idiot, this is your fault, so just get her to wake up!* God my inner voice can be such a bitch at times, but it doesn't make her any less right.

"And Dina's obviously been a bag of laughs since you...well you know," I finish lamely gesturing at the whole of her in the bed. "I think that Vamp has the hots for you. Please wake up soon, ok?" I whisper, before clearing a few errant strands from her face and leaving.

It's well past midnight when Dina appears in the small kitchen, scaring me shitless where I'm hunched over the worn kitchen table. "Fucking hell, could you not make a noise?"

"Why?" She asked, like appearing out of nowhere should have been a normal thing. "Has there been any change?" She asked, a little bit of hope flaring in her eyes.

"No, sorry she's still sleeping." I answered softly, noticing the light leaving her brown depths, and hating that I'd caused it.

"Ok, we'll be leaving in the morning, you should get some sleep." Dina mentioned before leaving me alone to my thoughts again.

What did she find out? I wondered as my eyes traced the empty doorway and my thoughts turned back to Lilah, where was she?

Tossing and turning all night on the small sofa, I was relieved when my alarm went off, the shrill beeps breaking the oppressive silence. I hadn't been able to shake the feeling that something really, really bad was about to happen. It had haunted me all night and continued even now as I rubbed at my tired eyes. *Fuck my life,* I thought swinging my legs off the side of the sofa and folding up the thin blanket I'd pulled off it's cushioned back.

"Morning sunshine," Jace's voice came from the kitchen. Of course he'd be up at this ungodly time.

"When have you ever called me sunshine?" I asked as I walked through the kitchen door, pinning him with my best death glare whilst he pottered about, making coffee on some complicated looking machine.

Ignoring my stare, Jace pushed a steaming mug of coffee my way, "I was hoping it might rub off on you, but clearly not." He said softly, still trying to get me back on friendly terms. "The coffee's really good by the way, Dina has an awesome Nespresso Machine," he said, nodding to my untouched mug.

"Have you spoken to Dina this morning?" I asked not wanting

to be left in silence again, and needing to know if we were actually going to move forward.

Jace opened his mouth, but it wasn't his voice that came out, "no he hasn't," Dina's sharp voice had me spinning on the spot, my coffee forgotten for now.

"So what happened last night?" I blurt out, too eager to wait.

"I managed to speak with a couple of my contacts in the city and the Scottish coven has been persecuted, more than any other throughout history, but stories have circulated over the years. We're going to Glasgow today." She explained to me as if I was a child, burrowing under my skin.

"Why Glasgow? I thought the witches were supposed to be here?" I ground out trying to keep my temper from flaring.

"There have been rumours of a witches coven up near Glasgow," Dina snaps before heading to the fridge and grabbing out a bag that looked suspiciously like a hospital blood bag.

"Seriously, is that blood?" I ask, disgust showing plainly in my voice as I watched her grab a cup up from the cupboard next to the fridge.

"What else would I be drinking?" *She responds flatly. She's a bloody vampire, stupid,* my inner voice chimes in sarcastically.

Opening my mouth, fully intending to give her a snarky remark, my eyes flash to Jace as he enters the conversation, "So when do we leave?" He asks, flashing me a quick head shake as he tries to keep the peace.

"In an hour," Dina explains, before leaving us both staring at a now empty spot.

Fuming, I snatched my almost cold coffee from the table and stamped my way to her guest room. I quickly changed into another set of comfy clothes, before searching my bag for a bobble. "For fuck sake." I declared to the empty room, as I realised if we didn't get to use a washing machine soon, I'd be running out of clean clothes in the next two days. Rummaging around in my bag, I grinned triumphantly when my fingers brushed a bobble, and I set about fixing my hair back.

I was sitting in the front room when Jace found me, staring

blankly at the opposite wall. "What's going on inside your head Ally?" He asked gently, taking a seat in one of the arm-chairs.

"Nothing much," I responded honestly, seeing no reason to lie, my head was about as worn out as I was with everything, "how long will it take to get to Glasgow?" I wondered aloud.

"About an hour, I think." He muttered, while slipping his phone from his pocket. "Yeah just over an hour depending on traffic." He answered glaring at his phone.

"Jace, do you really think that Lilah's alive and somewhere in Scotland?" I asked, giving voice to my worst fear.

"She has to be Ally," he stated, confidence radiating in his tone.

"Then why hasn't she found us?"

"I don't know Ally, only Lilah can tell us that." He replied, before we lapsed into a silence I let grow as I wondered what trouble Lilah might be in.

"Do you think Charleene will ever wake up?" I asked barely above a whisper, not wanting to upset Dina.

"You better pray that she wakes up."Dina spits from the doorway, where she cradles Charleene's unconscious form, "because if she doesn't then…"

"Don't finish that sentence unless you want a fight!" Jace snarls from his chair, cutting Dina's threat off, as he glared at her with murder in his eyes.

"Whatever, we're taking my car." Dina tossed at us before leaving, clearly expecting us to scramble after her.

"What's wrong with my car?" Jace called, springing to his feet.

"It's not mine," She stated flatly, already opening the front door.

"What about our stuff?" I called.

"It'll be fine here."

"But my car…" Jace began to disagree, with a wistful look at what had been his pride and joy since he'd bought it second hand.

"You can retrieve it when you come back this way, I'll help you shift your boxes into the house so we can get going." Dina offered, as she gently placed Charleene in one of the back passenger seats.

"Fine," Jace agreed, passing me his bag and unlocking his car.

Shifting all our boxes from Jace's boot into the house took under an hour with Dina and Jace's enhanced speed. I was currently wiggling on the smooth heated leather of the back seats of Dina's Audi, trying to get comfy next to Charleene, whose head now rested on a plump pillow. Smiling at her, I watch out the side window as Dina pulls away from the quiet street.

"Hello Princess." Lysais' silken voice makes me shiver and smile, as I open my eyes and stare at the meadow around me. Wild flowers are in full bloom, swaying in the gentle breeze that plays with my fiery red hair.

"Hey," I gasp, "what do you want?" I ask, knowing that this is a dream, from the idyllic meadow to the brilliant blue sky and my hair that looks like real flames as it blows across my face. I can even smell the sweet scent of Honeysuckle, Foxglove and Bluebells as they dance.

"I want you Princess," Lysais states, running his nose up the side of my neck as his strong arms enclose round me from behind. His unique scent of Leather and Lavender surrounds me, mixing with the wildflowers.

"Hmmm," I purr, unable to form a coherent thought.

"I want all of you." He growls in my ear, before his tongue darts out, licking from the bottom of my earlobe to the tip. I tremble against his arms as my legs threaten to give out. His smooth lips leave a trail of fire as they descend down my neck, making me squirm, "You're the only one for me."

Raised voices had me startling awake. "Absolutely not!" Dina yelled at Jace, without taking her eyes from the road ahead. It was loudest any of us had spoken while in Charleene's company.

"What the hell are you two arguing about now?" I asked around a yawn, as I rubbed the sleep from my eyes.

"Brainiac here wants to train your magic." Dina spat, glancing at me in the rear-view mirror.

"She needs to learn how to control it." Jace defended.

"Yeah, like that turned out so well last time." I scoff, before looking at Charleene's peaceful face, a stray strand of her dirty blonde hair falling across her peaceful face.

"You'll never get any better if you don't face it Ally." He explained, turning in his seat to give me his serious stare.

"Hmmm," I mumbled before watching the road flash by.

"We're almost at Glasgow, you can't have her letting off powerful magic in its limits," Dina mumbled, clearly giving up the fight.

"As soon as we reach a more remote place, I'm beginning her training." Jace begrudgingly agreed.

"Well, I'm so glad that's sorted." Charleene's calm voice made me jump out of my skin, as my head swiveled to stare at her. Dina slammed on the brakes, making us all fly forward against our seat-belts, to a chorus of angry car horns.

"What?" Charleene asked, unperturbed by the three sets of eyes staring unblinkingly at her.

"You're awake?" Dina whispered.

"Yes, I believe so." Charleene answered back, "so what was all that racket for?"

"Charleene, do you know what happened?" I asked tentatively.

"Yes," she states, looking at each of us in turn.

"Are you going to elaborate?" Jace asked carefully.

"I will, but not here. We're blocking traffic," she explains, while glancing behind us at the angry driver. "Where are we anyway?" She asked with a furrowed brow.

"We're almost at Glasgow," I let her know when it's clear Dina's not going to answer. " Dina do you need someone else to drive?" I nudge when she still hasn't moved.

"Nice one, I'm starvin'," Charleene says, making me chuckle. "How long?"

"Around 24 hours give or take a couple." I answer when no-one else pipes up.

"Oh." Charleene comments, then lapses into silence.

"Dina, drive the bloody car." Jace demands, giving her a small shake.

Slowly, like a statue coming back to life, Dina moves, putting the car in gear and slowly inching it forward, as more than one car horn blares behind us.

The rest of our drive to Glasgow passes uneventfully; both Charleene and Dina stay lost in their thoughts, and neither me or Jace break the silence. It's a relief when we pull up to a black wrought iron gate in the middle of nowhere. "So who owns this house?" I ask, my voice sounding very loud in the silent car.

"I do," Dina says, the first words she's uttered since Charleene first woke up. "It will be perfect for you to train and for Charleene to recover properly. It doesn't have any protective shields in place, but then that's not stopped what's-his-name from finding you before. So it'll have to do." She finishes as we pull up in front of the biggest house I've ever seen.

"Holy crap!" Charleene exclaims, as her gaze races along the massive Tudor style building, "you've been holding out on me." I could hear the wonder in her voice, as she pinned the back of Dina's head with a brief glare before her eyes returned to the building before us.

"Ok, well get comfy, I'm going into town this afternoon to speak with someone who might know where we can find the Nicnevin Coven. And I think it's You, Charleene that has been holding out on me! What the fuck happened back at Gladys'?"

"I hope you have food in there and tea," was Charleene's only response, leaving us all dumbfounded as she exited the car.

"The kitchen should be fully stocked, Mrs McClowd should be somewhere on the grounds," Dina replies as she stands in front of her sky blue car.

"You even have a freakin' housekeeper?" Charleene's excitement is infectious, as she bounces on the balls of her feet itching to get inside. I've missed her, I realise, as I look her over.

"We'll be talking about your…nap. And soon!" Dina reminds her, as she disappears inside.

"She's pretty pissed," Charleene states to no-one in particular when she's left with me and Jace.

"Well yeah, I'd be pretty pissed if Ally decided to go on a spirit walk and chose not to come back," Jace declared, before leaving both of us and following Dina.

"It was worth it though," Charleene whispered, as a flame burst to life above her palm.

"Holy shit girl!" I declare, studying the flame from every angle, marveling at the control and ease she wields it with. "What did you do, during your nap?" I asked, unable to help myself from reaching out my fingers and running them through it. "Fuck that's hot!" I shout as my finger tips barely make contact.

"Well duh! Ally you really shouldn't play with fire," Charleene laughs, making a giggle burst from my own throat, as she linked her arm through mine and explained all that had happened while she was asleep.

"I know where we'll find the Nicnevin Coven," she confided as we walked through the open front door together.

Trying to see anything that surrounded the cabin was impossible in the pitch black that had settled around us, but the lack of streetlights in the sky told me that this cabin of Dina's was remote. I mean, even our cottages had never been this remote and we'd been what normal folks called reclusive and weird! Turns out, Dina has many different hidey hole properties dotted all over the country, and even some in Europe and America.

Holding my breath, I take in the quiet of this place, before realising it's too quiet. The birds are silent, as though they've flown away all at once; even the small noises that insects make have died down to nothing, drawing my attention to the forest around our small meadow and cabin. Looking at the others, I see they've also noticed the eerie calm too. I'm about to ask what's happening when they appear out of nowhere. No warning, nothing. I watch, beginning to panic, as shadow after shadow comes alive.

"Shit," Dina's voice rings out in the fading light as she takes in what we're all seeing, "how the hell did they find us?" She asks, pushing Charleene behind her. I barely have time to shake my head, before a screech rips the night apart and others file in behind the Demoran. Quickly, my mind starts categorising them; vampires, witches, Fae. There's a battalion of creatures forming to attack us.

"There's too many," I gasp, as our clearing slowly fills, their howls and growls filling the night air. Shivering, I reach over grabbing daggers from the small bag next to me and stand facing off with the hoard before us. "Jace what do we do?" I ask through gritted teeth.

"We fight," he answers from my left, and I hear the swish of steel as he draws his own blade. My gaze flicks to him, taking in the determined set to his face as he assesses the situation we found ourselves in.

"Leave the vampires to me," Dina calls, before sprinting at them with a growl.

"I've got the witches." Charleene assures me, backing away to give herself room to move.

"We use everything we have against them." Jace says, glancing at me meaningfully, and I know what he wants me to do.

Shaking my head at him, "I can't," I tell him. He wants me to use my magic against them, "I'd hurt us as well as them."

"I believe in you Ally." He says before charging forward.

With no time left to prepare, I lose a breath, reaching inside myself for that strange quiet place I've found. The place inside my mind where I stop thinking altogether and just let my instincts take over. Snarling, I charge in behind Jace, my daggers finding arteries, necks, faces—any place that draws blood—as I think *I'm going to need something more than daggers.*

Spinning around, searching for Jace amongst the bodies crowding around me, I see a witch with her back to me aiming a spell towards where we left Charleene. Blood splatters my face as my dagger plunges in and out of her neck, before she even knows

I'm behind her.

"Gatemaker," growls a Demoran, "you're mine pretty." It grunts, over-confident before charging towards me.

"Hey ugly," I laugh, flicking the blood from my hands, waiting for it to draw closer. I don't know who this person is that I've become, as excitement floods through me. Dodging his shadow sword I dart in, nicking his side with my dagger, making him grunt as he turned to keep me in his line of sight.

My smile falters for a second as it lets out a broken growling sound, that I realise is laughter. "I think I'll keep you as mine," it tells me, slowly advancing on me again, backing me away from the battle.

"You wish," I snap, darting towards him with my dagger aimed at where its heart should be. Plunging the blade hilt deep, I snarl in frustration as it just laughs at me again. Fuck, these bastards are hard to kill. Abandoning my dagger, I lunge back away from its claws, dropping to the floor and rolling past it, coming up to my feet. I realise it's succeeded in separating me as the trees close around us.

Damn it, I shout in my head, as I recognise my mistake. Panic tries to edge into my killing calm but I force it away, knowing I'm dead if I let it take over. We can't be far from the clearing as I can still hear the growls and screams from the battle waging there. For a moment I wonder who's winning, us or them, before I push those thoughts from my mind, as I feel it.

My magic. It's simmering below my skin, wanting to get out. Gritting my teeth together, but not taking my focus from the Demoran before me, I try shoving my power back inside the box I keep it in, as the Demoran dissolves into the shadows around us.

"Poor little Princess, all alone," the Demoran taunts, it's voice seeming to come from everywhere, breaking my concentration on my magic. Fear floods me as it bubbles closer to the surface. "Mmmmm, your fear's delicious" it growls, appearing nearer to me, forcing me to take another step backwards.

Fear courses through me as I realise I'm not going to be able to contain it any longer. Who am I going to hurt? I wonder as I take another step back, and my back slams into a tree, knocking the air from my lungs as the Demoran laughs at me before disappearing again.

Suddenly it appears right in front of me, making me scream as I swipe with my last remaining dagger. It evades my attack easily, disappearing into the shadows again as I realise it's playing with me. My eyes widen as I feel it's cold, clammy hand close around my throat from behind, cutting off my oxygen before it makes itself solid, pushing me away from the tree as I try to scratch at its wrist.

"I've caught a prize indeed," it's voice grating on my ear drums, as its thumb strokes the column of my throat. Shivering at the cold emanating from it, my eyes dart around me searching for a friend to save me. "You're all alone now." It states, making my panic flare.

Grabbing at its wrist, I try pulling its hand from my neck as dark spots start blocking out my vision. If I don't breathe soon I'm going to die, I realise a split second before I reach inside myself. My mind acts quickly, searching out the elemental magic coursing through me, grabbing at the power in my blood and forcing it out through my hands.

Light blinds me, as fire races from my hands, coating the Demoran in seconds. His screams deafen me as I grab hold of his arm, holding him to me as my power burns him. His struggles against my hold begin to falter, and then they fail altogether as the smell of burnt paper invades my nose, making me want to sneeze as the Demoran turns to ash.

What the hell? I ask myself, staring at my now normal looking hands, the magic actually did what I wanted for a change.

The distant noises from the clearing break through my shock, reminding me that the others are still fighting. Running as fast as I can, I notice the trees as dark blurs, barely registering the drop in temperature or the snow that's falling as I draw nearer to the clearing.

"Hey Princess," Lysias' deep growl stops me dead. Looking forward, I'm just steps from the clearing, "miss me beautiful?"

He asks, making me shiver as his voice washes over me. Turning slowly, I face him as he appears amongst the trees.

"Nope," I lie, letting my mouth pop on the p, watching as frustration at my games plays across his face, "I remember who you are to me." I tell him inching closer.

"Really?" He asks back smiling, "I highly doubt that beautiful."

A snarl from the clearing has my head snapping round on my neck, it's still full of creatures, all attacking my friends, "stop this?" I whisper, turning back watching him for any change in his stoic mask, if I'd expected anything I would have been disappointed as he stares at me.

"What, and stop my fun? I don't think so beautiful." He sneers at me, making me gasp as his cruel words settle in my brain.

"What happened to you?" I scream at him, trying to understand the stranger I see before me.

"I woke up," he snaps, before disappearing and reappearing in front of my face, his hand closing around my neck.

"I loved you," I gasp out, confused, searching his dull eyes as he laughs at me.

"You really did," he mocks, his eyes flicking over my shoulder before returning to my face, "but I never loved you." He sneers at me as I feel Jace appear behind me.

"Let her go!" Jace growls at him, taking a step forward until my hand stops him.

"Stop this Ly?" I ask again, as tears fill my eyes, but I refuse to look away. "Come back to me Ly," I whisper as dark spots appear over my vision.

"I can't!" Ly growls, throwing me through the air. My breath leaves my lungs as I fly into the raging battle.

Taking deep breaths I push myself to my feet, glancing around as Demoran rise up. Spinning around, I try to settle my racing heart as I realise Ly has just signed my death warrant.

Jace flashes past me in a blur, clashing with the Shadow man who was poised to attack me—protecting me again—as another rises up from the dark to my left, aiming for my head. Falling backwards slightly, I feel the blade cut through the air where my neck had just been. *Shit, this is real Ally!* I scream at myself before letting go of all my rational thoughts. I let Her take over. Alysium. The other me dodges each attack, waiting for an opening that she can use as another shadow man joins the fight. I'm kicking and punching, but I no longer have a weapon as I try protecting myself. I feel my magic rise inside me again, but fear has me battling it back down.

Not here, not now, I think to myself, shaking my hands. I know Ly's still here, I can feel his eyes watching me as I defend myself. I feel the flames circle my hands but I realise I'm out of options as I jump backwards, snarling as I barely dodge another sword aimed at my right arm.

The decision made, I draw my fire to me, praying that no one I care about gets hurt. I hear Jace grunting somewhere close by, fighting his own battles as I try to keep all of my attackers in view. I watch as they swarm Jace, keeping him from me. We might not be too friendly at the minute, but he was still like a brother to me. Fury washes through me and I lose it.

On a scream I let my power free, smiling briefly as fire and ice fly from me, striking anyone stupid enough to be standing in the clearing. Air rushes around me, forcing Jace—Dina and Charleene too I hope—away to the safety of the tree line as I finally let myself go. Power pulses out from me in waves, cleansing the clearing of all the monsters who haven't already run from my wrath. I'm standing in the center of the whirlwind, my mind going numb. I look back, meeting Ly's gaze as my magic begins to settle.

"I'll be coming for you beautiful," His voice reaches me before he smiles and winks, cloaking himself in a swirl of shadows.

"Alyssa!" Jace's terrified scream has me turning, confused, just as my breath is stolen from the punch to my back. Glancing behind me, I let my magic freeze the stray Demoran who's standing behind me, before turning back to Jace across the clearing.

"Jace," I try saying, but all that comes out is a gurgling sound, as I taste metal on my tongue. As my eyes finally register the blade sticking out of my stomach just below my rib cage. I begin to feel the pain split me in half but I can't scream, can't move as the ebony blade holds me up. Then everything speeds up Jace flashes to me, as the blade slides backwards.

I feel every inch of it leave my body, slicing through muscle and skin, locking eyes with Jace. I barely register Dina's worried voice or the snow that's now falling around us. All I can focus on is Jace's eyes, gasping for air as my knees turn to jelly and I fall to the floor. Gasping like a fish, I watch in disbelief as my blood begins bubbling from below my ribcage and splattering the ground, slowly turning the crisp white snow red.

Jace's warm arms close around me as he lifts me into his lap, brushing stray strands of my hair from my face, "I've got you Ally," he whispers over and over as I give in to the darkness blocking my sight. The last thing I remember is an animalistic growl shattering the silence.

Chapter Twenty-One

Lysais.

"What the fuck did you make me do?" I growl at the room, making the dirty windows shake, as Balor backs away from the seething anger I'm directing his way. All I see is Ally's perfect face, distorted first in confusion that morphed quickly to horror, as my hand launched her across the blood soaked field. *My hand did that to her!* My traitorous mind screams at me, as I look in horror at said hands.

"I never meant for that to happen." He cautiously explains, still backing up towards the opposite wall as I stalk forward.

"You killed her!" I growl as my chest splits in two, at my failure to protect her and at the prospect of my Ally no longer being in the land of the living. She had so much before her, so much to do before her time should have come. Fuck this war. I rage inside my mind, my gaze pinned on the sniveling form of 'my brother' as he cowers. This is why Father hasn't acknowledged him, I didn't even know he existed until they forced the shadow bond on my mind. "He wanted her alive, not skewered on a sword." I continue without him answering, delighting in the way he flinches.

"I know, she wasn't supposed to get stabbed!" Balor yells back at me, letting his frustration at the situation show. With his words I watch again as the sword pierces her stomach from behind, seeing the moment she realised what had happened. I feel my body moving far too slowly, as her knees give out and she falls to the floor, her blood soaking her jumper. My growl still reverberated in my ears as her eyes closed.

"What about the bond?" He questions me. "Lysais, can you still feel the damn bond you two have?" His fearful words finally drag me back to the here and now. Could I still feel our bond? I wonder, trying to find that warm spark that normally resides inside my cold chest. Searching, I lose all hope as I fail to find it.

"No, no, no!" I wail to the room, he's brought us to.

"I'm guessing that's a no." Balor's cold voice raises my hackles even further. She was one of the only good things left in my life, and he'd forced me to execute her , in his damn quest to drag her to cower at Father's feet.

"You fucking Twat," I scream pushing all of my hate and pain into my voice as it rings around the room. Shadows dance up and down my arms as my magic raises around me, pushing into my head and dampening his hold on me.

His eyes widen, terrified as I Lunge at him, ready to wring his good-for-nothing throat.

Chapter Twenty-Two

Jacin.

"Alysium!" I scream as a Demoran rears up behind her, it's sword raised. She turns, confused for a moment as my shout distracts her. Frozen to the spot, I watch as the sword shoves through her middle and pokes out through her stomach. Nausea rolls in my gut as her body sways slightly, and I feel her magic stir as she glances at the Demoran behind her, forcing him to stop dead. Then she's meeting my gaze again as her mouth opens, silently saying my name.

Beside me Lysais is as frozen as I am, obviously happy with how his plan worked out. She was the key to everything back home; she'd been sent here to protect her from him, and look how that'd turned out. I can't take my eyes off her as she glances down, her dark blue eyes widening slightly as she realises what's just happened to her. My feet finally remember how to work as I sprint towards her, I barely reach her before her magic wears off and the fucking Demoran slides his blade free, with a sickening sucking sound as more of Alyssa's blood follows it.

Her mouth is still trying to form words as blood sprays from her onto the ground. Snow begins to fall in a blizzard, covering the blood stained field in a blanket of pure white; *it's too innocent a colour for what's happened here*, I think as, my arms close around Ally and drag her to my chest. "I've got you Ally," I whisper, clearing the errant strands of her unruly red hair from her face as her eyes roll back into her head.

No! My mind screams, as it tries to split in two. An animalistic growl, like nothing I'd ever heard before, splits the air behind me but I don't even glance His way. Whatever pain he's feeling won't be nearly enough for what he's just done. I'm going to kill the bastard if I ever see him again.

"Jace?" Charleene's quiet voice drags my attention away from Ally's peaceful face, "Jacin, she's still breathing." Her words breathe life into me as I carefully watch Alyssa's chest. It rises barely, but it still rises. I stamp down on the sudden hope that flares to life in my chest. That was a mortal wound, especially since Ally has no access to her Fae healing. I can't hope yet, it would kill me.

"Guys, I think you should see this," Dina says carefully from somewhere behind me. Glancing at her, my head swivels as I look in the same direction she's staring. There, across the now empty field, a short plump woman is striding purposefully towards us.

"I told you they would find us here," Charleene mutters happily, before turning back to me and holding me in her chocolate gaze, "Jacin she's going to be ok."

Chapter Twenty-Three

Alyssa.

Running, I smell the freesia and pomegranates of the gardens before I see them as I push through the heavy iron gate, making it screech. Anticipation makes my feet move faster, as excitement floods through me. Ly's been away again, but he's finally back today and I can't wait to see him. I follow the tug on my heart as I make my way through each garden, then out onto the small path running by the palace. I'm almost there, I can see the gates to the statue garden before me.

His note sounded urgent, but I don't care as long as I can see him. I'm like a giddy child at Yule time as I force myself to go faster. Barreling noisily through the gates, I run down the paths, not slowing as I see him.

"Lysias!" I call breathlessly as I throw myself at his chest, "never leave me again." I mumble against the smooth leather that covers his chest.

"Princess," he greets the top of my head before pushing me away from him, "we need to talk."

"I don't care about talking Ly," I mumble, fighting against his strength so I can stay close to him.

"Alysium this is important!" He stresses but I don't want to hear him as I shake my head. "My Father is preparing something big, I couldn't find out what it is but he was excited. I've never seen him this excited, ever."

"Hey, whatever it is, we'll face it together." I smile up at him trying to calm him down.

"I need to go back." His eyes lock with mine, and I see the indecision waring in them, "Father wants me back."

I know he still wants his father's approval and how much he hates that part of himself, "your Mother sent you here to keep you safe Ly, she did that for a reason."

"I know that, but he's still my Father. Maybe I can reach him, make *him see sense."*

I hear the sadness in his voice as it wobbles, and think about how I'd feel if it was my Father that was an insane king, obsessed with conquering another realm, and realise I would want to try too. "I understand," I murmur, even as I feel the pain splitting me in two.

"I need to try and help my family as well, I can't leave her suffering any longer."

"How bad has it got?" I ask, already knowing he won't tell me, at his sad head shake I ask another question, "when will you leave?"

"I don't know when he'll send for me again," He says brokenly, and I know we won't have much longer together.

Blinking in the bright sunshine flooding in through a near-by window I flinched, remembering the blade that was stuck through my middle only moments before. Was it only moments? I wondered, absently rubbing my stomach as I looked around. I'm alone in a house I realise, staring at the four walls around me, but who's house? Lysias' cruel gaze suddenly flashes before my eyes, the hate and disgust I saw right before he threw me into the middle of that field has me seeing red.

"Where the fuck is he?" I roar at the empty room, and the door almost breaks off its hinges as Jace comes flying through it, faster than I've ever seen him move.

"You're awake," he states the obvious, while looking me over as if he can see through the covers to my body beneath.

"Where?" I ask again, in a more reasonable but deadly calm tone, making Jace stiffen.

"Gone." Is the only answer he gives me, as he turns his furious gaze out the window staring down at something I can't see from my bed.

"Where are we?" I ask, glancing around the unfamiliar room again.

"You're safe," a familiar voice, a voice that I haven't heard in almost two months, floats over to me from the doorway that Jace came through moments ago. Stunned, my head snaps towards the sound, meeting Lilah's familiar hazel eyes as my heart seems to stop beating for a second, before it kicks back in, doubling its pace.

"Lilah," I gasp as a weight I hadn't even known I was carrying seems to lift from my shoulders. Running my eyes over every inch of her, I try to make sure she's all in one piece and really here, "are you real?" I ask not believing my eyes.

"I am," she confirms with a smile, as I run my eyes over her again.

"What happened to you? How did you end up here? Where is here?" All my questions run into each other in my haste to get every word out, making her smile as she comes and sits on the edge of the bed next to me.

"The important question is how are you Ally?" Her voice drops as her eyes flit over my covered stomach.

"I'm..." I pause, not willing to lie and say I'm fine when I'm not, "confused." I finally find the right word to sum up how I feel, as my hand caresses the smooth skin across my stomach, there's not even a scar.

"Understandably," Lilah glances at Jace's back, before returning her gaze to me. "How much do you know already?" She asks, watching me closely.

"Not much, I can use magic but don't know why," I begin to explain as succinctly as I can, "I know that I'm Fae, are you one too? I know I should probably be dead but I'm clearly not? And I've met..." I trail off remembering how hostile Jace gets around Lysias and how angry Lysais had been at me in the clearing.

"You've met who honey?" Lilah's calm tone brings tears to my eyes as I realise just how much I've missed her.

"She's met him!" Jace spits from the window, speaking for the first time since Lilah entered.

"Why do you hate him so much?" I ask exasperated with him, but when I glance at Lilah I see the colour has vanished from her face as she watches me carefully.

"Because he's evil, or did him throwing you into the middle of a battle not clue you into that Ally?" His tone bites as he snaps at me.

"I...I..." I can't answer him. Even though I know I should hate Ly, I can't.

"No Ally, do not even try to defend him. You're so wrapped up in him that you still can't see what everyone else can, no matter what he does to you!" The venom in Jace's voice forces me to physically draw back, like a slap to the face, before he storms from the room.

"Jace..." I try to stop him from leaving but sobs strangle my throat and all I can do is watch him leave.

"Don't worry Ally, he'll come around." Lilah's calm voice wraps around me, making my tears fall.

"I've missed you," I blurt out before wrapping my arms around her and squeezing. We do nothing for a few minutes, as she lets me cry against her shoulder whilst she brushes her hand against my hair. It's so familiar that it causes more tears to fall. "Who am I?" I ask quietly.

"You're special," I hear the smile in her voice without needing to look at her as she tells me I'm special for what must be the millionth time since I met her. "You have a block on your memories Sweetheart, one that was placed there with very strong magic, and only strong magic will be able to break it for you. But you have to be ready." With the last of her speech, I draw back to look at her in disbelief, ready to laugh, but her serious stare halts me.

"Why?" Is the only question I can think to ask now.

"To protect you, to keep you hidden." I can see she wants to tell me more but I also notice as she closes off from me like Jace does when he's not sure the information won't hurt me, and I realise maybe I've been a little unfair to him. All he's ever done is try to protect me.

"So my life is made from magic and lies," I sigh, "how do we break it?"

"There are some witches here that are willing to try, but I won't lie anymore Ally, it's going to be painful."

Gulping down my fear, I try smiling as I nod my agreement. I need to be free of it, to know myself properly whoever I was or, I suppose, am? "Okay," I agree quietly.

"Do you want to talk about it, Ally?" She's patient, waiting for me to think through if I want to tell her or not. She's never pushed me before, and I doubt she's about to start now.

"He's different," is all I get out before the tears start falling down my cheeks, "I remember him being kind to me, I even thought he loved me Lilah." I sob as she envelopes me in one of her motherly hugs.

"Oh my sweet girl, I can't say much but people change all the time and we don't know everything." Her tone is motherly as she rubs my back, "Only you know how your heart feels."

"But what if Jace is right and he's evil, how can I love such a monster?" I cry, trying to match the two versions of the man I love together.

Clinging to Lilah I almost miss what she says next over my sobs, "not all monsters are monstrous to everyone." Her voice is soft, almost like she's remembering something of her own as she comforts me.

"You really think so?" I ask timidly, pulling away from her slightly so I can look at her face.

"I do,"she says smiling sadly at me, "but that doesn't mean they get to hurt my sweet girl." She says fiercely as she cups my cheek, making me laugh,"That's better, now you need to rest." And I know there'll be no arguing with her, so I settle back against the pillows.

"I'm sorry we didn't get to you in time. Will you tell me what happened?" I ask, although my eyelids are already heavy and I begin drifting off into a dreamless sleep, listening to her familiar voice as she explains how she escaped and how she ended up where-ever the hell here is.

Groggily I blink my eyes open, staring at the now dark window, as my mind slowly pieces everything together again, the fight, my wound, waking up here safe and whole...LILAH! My mind screams as I'm already flinging back the covers and running for the door. Just as my fingers brush the smooth wood, I realise I have no idea what this house will be like, or where I'll even find her. All I know is that I need to make sure it hadn't been a dream and that Lilah was really alive and well.

"Lilah?" I whisper as I walk down the small hallway and find a set of stairs leading down. "Lilah?" It's like a mantra as I take each step slowly, "Lilah," step, "Lilah," step "Lilah," step, "Lilah?" I know my voice is barely audible, but I'm also not surprised when Jace finds me on the last step.

"You should be resting." He dead pans at me with a slight quirk to his eyebrow.

"Lilah?" I whisper back at him, he nods once before turning and leading me outside.

"She's ok Ally," Jace reassures me as I pause on the thresh-hold, looking at the street before me. There's a row of maybe twelve houses, all made of wood. Some had lights on and others were dark and there, sitting on a small porch opposite ours, was Lilah. My breathing returns to normal as her eyes meet mine and I can trust that it wasn't a dream.

"Alyssa, come here sweetheart," Her voice is soft but I hear it all the same as I cross the small street, pausing at the bottom of her steps. "Sit with me." She invites before I find myself slowly climbing the steps.

"Where are we?" I ask, the moment my arse hits the bench next to her.

"I wondered how much you'd remember when you woke up, we're with the oldest coven of witches."

"Hmmmm," I mumble, not letting my eyes wander from hers.

"I believe you've been looking for them, your friend is related to the elders of this coven."

"Charleene found her family?" I ask before I can stop myself.

"She has my child, just as you have found the rest of yours." Lilah's smile makes me break and anger slips into my tone.

"But have I?" I ask and watch as her face falls.

"Well, almost dear," Lilah replies sadly.

"Please tell me what happened? Who are they? Why would they send me here?"

"That's a long, complicated answer and one that I can't give you right now," she pauses letting me gather myself, "but I've asked the elders here if they can help with your memory issues and the block on your mind."

I look at her, bewildered and gobsmacked that she would have even asked this already. "Why?" Is again the only question I can think to ask.

"Jace has told me of your journey, and the battles you've faced. You need to know your past in order to face your future, whatever that may be." Her cryptic answer has me smiling again, it's such a Lilah way of answering my doubts and fears.

"And what have they said, the elders I mean?"

"That they will deliberate, meet with you and then decide if they can help."

"Oh..." I answer back, feeling a little dejected that my future lay in the hands of a group of women that had abandoned a baby. "Ok." I answer Lilah when I realise she's waiting for more from me. "I need to know more Lilah, what happened to you?" I ask again, waiting for the same answers everyone's been giving me lately and that's nothing.

"Alyssa, I need you to listen to me clearly when I tell you this because I will not be repeating myself." Lilah's stern voice almost makes me smile, before nodding for her to continue. "Ok so the night I disappeared, Lysais came to our cottage. He chased me through to the bedroom where I managed to escape him. I used my magic," she pauses, letting my mind process her words and to see if it would react before she went on. "It was set up to bring me to the most powerful magical beings on this world, and it brought me quite literally to the feet of the Nicnevin Coven."

"But why didn't you try to find us?" I ask the most burning question inside me.

"If I had Ally, neither you or Jace would have discovered all that you have, or become the two people I see before me now. I can't fight all of your battles for you." She answered with a smirk.

"Fair enough," I mumble, not wanting her to be right as always.

"Look at you, Ally, you have become this beautiful, confident and strong young woman. You took a sword to the stomach and still managed to keep fighting." I couldn't help but smile at that assessment, even if I didn't completely feel that way.

"If you say so." I agree, not wanting to argue, "so what do I need to know about the Nicnevin Coven?" I asked, not ready to leave her side just yet.

Chapter Twenty-Four

Alyssa.

"Alyssa," Charleene's high voice shouts, as she almost runs in the front door, finding me sprawled out on the sofa reading yet another book off of the shelves lining the front room. "Come on." She laughs before grabbing my hand and pulling me up, "tonights the night!"

"What's tonight?" I ask as she drags me from the house me and Jace have been staying in, since the coven took all of us in a week ago.

"The winter solstice! And apparently, that means celebrating," She says with a smirk and wink as I groan, "dancing, drinking," She explains bumping me with her hip, before shoving me towards the door.

"I'm not going." I grumble as she pushes me out into the street, if you can even call it a street. Each building is made of wood, the same as ours, plain and simple with enough rooms to suit the occupants needs, but easy to get rid of in a hurry if needed. The whole coven was the same, all ready to up and move at a moment's notice if need be. I suppose that's what comes from being persecuted and hunted for as long as the Nicnevin witches have. They tended not to trust very easily, from what Lilah's told us, I can understand why.

"Oh yes you are," She states, breaking into my thoughts as she pushes me over the threshold and into someone else's hands, "and you need a dress."

Groaning, I meet the eyes of Charleene's newest friend Sophia's, briefly taking in the conspiring smirk as the two of them push and pull me upstairs into what must be Sophia's bedroom. I'm greeted by a sea of white—every inch of the bed is taken up with white dresses. Groaning louder, I jump at the bang as Charleene shuts the door behind us and I mentally check out as they talk about tonight and the celebrations planned, letting them pull dresses over my head and oohing and ahhing at each one.

Urg, I hate big gatherings, always have if my dreams are anything to go by. It's one of the things that makes *me*, I guess. Thinking of my latest dream with Lysais has me blushing.

"And what is that blush for?" Sophia's high-pitch voice breaks into my thoughts, making me blush harder. Glancing between her and Charleene, I can see neither of them are going to let it go until I tell them.

"I had another dream last night," I mutter watching as they both draw nearer, shaking my head as I give in. Smiling, I realise I like having girlfriends, as much as Charleene and Sophia are girlfriends of mine, and I explain every detail to them.

"And Lysais is the hottie that keeps springing up and putting you in danger?" Sophia asks, fanning her face as though it's on fire.

"Yep," I say, popping the 'p'.

"Why?" Sophia asks, looking at me like she's trying to figure out a complex puzzle.

"Why what?" I ask, genuinely confused.

Giggling and blushing even more, it takes Sophia a moment to compose herself before explaining her question, "I mean if he likes you, why does he keep putting you in danger?" Her question seems simple enough, but I'll be damned if I know.

"He wants something," Charleene states, watching my reaction. I mean fair play- I'm not the most level headed when it comes to Ly. "He's been hunting you Ally." She goes on patiently.

"Well he made it obvious at the clearing that it's not me that he wants, so am I being hunted?" I ask, remembering his cold, calculated words, before he literally threw me away. Letting out a sigh, I watch as Sophie and Charleene exchange a glance, "What? What now?" I demanded they share what that damn look was about!

"Well... maybe he needs you specifically for something, even if he doesn't want you." I feel the pain, even as I shrug, trying not to let her words burrow into my head and heart.

"Okay," Sophia says, clapping to get our attention, "this is too depressing, and we need to find you both dresses for tonight. There's only one place that we'll be able to get you anything, even halfway decent. Rosie's place." Sophia explains bouncing with excitement, making me and Charleene groan together.

Rosie's Place, as it turns out, is a one story wooden house with two main rooms, a small kitchen and a bathroom that doubled as a changing room. The first room was filled with rack after rack of dresses, shirts, jeans and other clothes, all reigned over by a small hurricane of a women. Rosie was a fiery redhead, with startling green eyes that bored into me, as she cooed over our good looks and slight frames.

In the end, we both ended up with white dresses for the winter solstice celebrations. "Have you spoken to the elders?" Rosie asked conversationally as she helped me pick out—in her words not mine—the perfect dress.

"Erm no," I answered honestly, wondering what the elders were like. All I knew about them so far is that they're Charleene's Mother, Grandmother and her younger sister Angelinia.

"Well child, I heard they were looking to speak to you," she paused, looking me over again, "and I wouldn't keep them waiting if I were you." Her voice was motherly and warm, making me like her just a little bit.

"Ok I won't," I mutter, not wanting to get close to anyone here. We'd be leaving at some point.

"You all done?" Sophia's perky voice has me jumping out of my skin.

"Yeah, I think so?" I ask, glancing at Rosie as she dominates the room.

"She's done 'ere," Rosie confirms, letting me out to join Sophia and Charleene as they bounce around the small shop, "but you make sure she visits with the Maiden, Mother and Crone, Sophia McCallister." She threatens before we can leave the shop.

"Yes Ma'am," Sophia responds like it's second nature.

"What do they want to see you for?" Charleene asks curiously as she glances up and down the road.

"About tonight I guess," I mumble, only half paying attention, as I glare down the road towards the biggest hut in town. "Aren't they supposed to be your family or something?" I query, unable to stop the question from blurting out.

"Or something alright." And it was Charleene's turn to glare at the hut.

"Come on, you two, they're not that bad. I mean yeah, us witches can be a little old school, but overall this Coven's pretty ok," Sophia informs us with what I now know is her usual smile. "If they have Rosie watching out for you Ally, then it would be best to get it over and done with," she says, going to link arms with Charleene, and looking a little hurt when Charleene steps away.

"I'll come with you, I should really hear what they have to say to me at some point."

Nodding, I turn and follow the road towards the hut at the end, its arching doorway, "So anything I should know before we walk in there?" I ask, barely above a whisper.

"Well, Aradia-the woman who's supposed to be my mother, she seems nice enough but also kind of reserved. It turns out she didn't want to give me up but her mother, my Grandmother Agnes, made her choose." Confused, my eyes meet Charleene's beneath her furrowed brow.

"Are you fucking joking me?" I state offended on Charleene's behalf, "your grandmother made your mother give you up? Why would anyone do that?" I ask, forgetting all about the stupid prophecy Gladys spoke of.

"So I was the older twin of two girls," Charleene explains, "Grandmother took me and gave me away to one orphanage and my twin sister was given to another, Angelinia is Mother's third child to a man of the Coven, Grandmother wouldn't tell me who my father was." I could hear the hurt as plain as day in Charleene's voice, and decided I'd heard enough.

"Well they want to go magically poking around in my head," I blurt out, trying to lighten the mood and failing.

"I'm sure they're very skilled, all three of them, and with my spirit walk I didn't turn out too bad in the end." Smiling, she shoulder bumped me, forcing me to smile too.

Charleene hadn't told me and Jace exactly what had happened in her 'spirit walk' but, from what I've seen, she'd had her magic awakened, and received a very thorough history lesson on the Nicnevin Coven and where we had needed to be to make her vision come to pass of them finding us. "So what's the story with scary Vamp face guy?"

"Oh him! Well apparently you're not the only one who's in hot demand by evil men." She answered cryptically before switching the subject, "they should be able to fix your head Ally, but isn't the chance to know everything you're missing worth the risk?"

"I suppose so, it's still weird to have a group of people messing inside your head." I argue, just as we stop at the meeting hut door.

Chapter Twenty-Five

Alyssa.

Groaning, I glance at the white dress hanging on my door. It's made of a thin soft material that hugs my curves before floating out until it reaches the floor. Charleene and Sophia assured me that it was required for tonight's ceremony.

The coven had agreed to try and remove the block in my head, tonight at the winter equinox, as their powers would be stronger. It was all the coven members could talk about so I'd retreated into my room to hide from all the mutterings. Sighing, I tried to return my attention to the book Sophia had lent me, but I couldn't focus on the words as my mind churned with questions about what tonight would unlock.

Would I finally have answers to why my memories and powers had been sealed? I hoped so, as the puzzle was driving me crazy. Almost as crazy as Lysais' erratic behaviour. One minute he was cold and distant, then the next he was warm and protective. It was like there were two of him, both completely different.

Urg! I groaned, turning on my side and staring out the small window, watching as the sky began to change colour. It was beautiful as the sky changed from blue to red, looking like it was on fire as my heart sank knowing that I'd have to get ready soon.

The ritual wouldn't begin until midnight, but the celebrations were due to begin at seven. Looking at the dress once more, I let out a sigh before dragging myself to the bathroom. It was small; just a toilet, sink and a bathtub with a shower over it. Walking over to the bath, I turned on the hot water tap and let it run until it was hot, before putting the plug in.

Leaving the water running, I looked at myself in the small mirror over the sink. Taking in my porcelain skin and blue eyes, I tried to see something different in them. *I should look different, shouldn't I?* I thought to myself, as steam slowly covered over my reflection, reminding me of the bath running. Shaking my head at my silly thoughts, I turned my attention to adding enough cold water before stripping out of my clothes, holding my breath and sinking below the water.

The heat soothed the muscles I hadn't even known I was tensing, as I let myself think about tonight's ritual. The witches, including Charleene, would surround me as they called upon their ancestors to help them unlock the spell on my mind. It was too strong for one witch to do alone, with it being a full blooded Fae that had placed the block on me. The Council of Elders had explained to me that it might be painful, but that I mustn't fight it as my instincts would scream at me to do.

Both Jace and Lilah thought this was the best way; I needed to return home eventually and, until the spell was gone, I wouldn't be able to open the gate. My lungs began to hurt as I opened my eyes, staring up at the distorted ceiling. Banging interrupted my quiet, even if it was muted below the water. Breathing out, I let go of all my worries as air bubbles float to the surface, before letting my head break the water and gasping in a lungful of air.

"What?" I shout at the door, annoyed at whoever it was for breaking the calm I'd been working on creating inside my head. God knows I'd need to be calm tonight.

"Ally?" Lilah's voice came through the door, "You ok hun?" Her concern quieted my anger slightly, as I reminded myself of all she gave up to protect me.

"I'm fine Lilah, I'll be out in a minute." I answer, scrubbing my skin with the bar of floral smelling soap and turning the shower on to wash my hair. Once I'd shampooed and conditioned my long curls, I wrapped myself up in towels and braced myself before walking back to my room.

"Ah here she is," Lilah's voice made me smile as I took in her strained smile, before turning to Charleene's grinning face.

"You ready?" She asks, waiting for my nod, before pulling me fully into my room. "Good, we don't have much time." She mutters before shoving the white dress at me and ushering Lilah for the room so I could change.

After drying every inch of my body I pulled on a pair of clean white lace knickers, before sliding the dress over my head. It left my shoulders bare, the thin sleeves starting halfway down my upper arms and flowing down to cover my hands. They weren't needed as the corset of the dress was strong enough to hold it up, while pushing up and supporting my breasts.

Sighing, I turned to the full length mirror as Lilah and Charleene returned, both gasping at the sight of me. I looked different, as the corset pulled in my stomach and the dress hugged my hips, showcasing them before it flared out towards the ground. Tiny clear beads caught the light when I moved, making the whole dress sparkle.

"I look stupid," I mumble to them, meeting Lilah's eyes in the mirror.

"Don't be daft," Charleene answers, shaking her head at me as I turn my gaze to her. "You just need some finishing touches," She explains before muttering a string of Latin. I watch in amazement as my hair dries into tight ringlets, magically twisting two thin braids on either side of my head that pinned delicately in place at the back.

It's simple, but the braids keep my curls from falling into my face. Charleene dips into the bag on my bed that I hadn't noticed and threads something around my head before securing it at the back where the braids meet. "Sit," she demands, pointing at a chair away from the mirror. Glancing between Lilah's shining eyes and Charleene's determined expression, I gave up any complaints I was going to make and sat in the chair.

"Now close your eyes," With one last pleading look at Lilah, I do as I'm told and sit quietly as Charleene applies some make-up. I'm almost falling asleep as she announces, "there, you're done!"

Opening my eyes, I stare at the face looking back at me in the small hand mirror Lilah's holding up and gasp. Charleene has worked wonders; my eyelids are dusted with a shimmering dark blue power that looks like the night sky has been painted across them. The eyeliner is a work of art, sweeping across my lids to join with an elegant pattern of swirls that frame my eyes, creating a painted mask around my upper face. My lips look full and have been painted a bright red that matches my hair.

A thin band of silver holds a string of what look like snowdrops against my forehead, but as they catch the light rainbows shine inside them. Reaching up, I gingerly touch the crystals, knowing I look confused as Lilah wipes a tear from her cheek. "It was your mothers," she whispers.

"Are they diamonds?"

Lilah nods as Charleene squeals in delight, "do you like it?" All I can do is nod and smile, as I look at myself in the mirror.

"I look..." *like a princess* I finish off in my head, not wanting to voice the thought.

"You look like you always should have, Ally." Lilah says with motherly love before wiping another tear away.

"Is all of this necessary though?" I ask, grimacing at how fancy I look for a ritual.

"Absolutely," Charleene giggles, "it's a party Ally, let your hair down and maybe you-know-who will turn up," she says, wiggling her eyebrows and making me snort.

"Hmmmm," I respond

"See ya there," she says, kissing my cheek and bouncing out of my room. Shaking my head, I look at myself one last time before turning to Lilah.

"You're not wearing white," I grumble as I take in the black dress she's wearing.

"I'm not taking part in the ritual so I don't need to." She answers patiently.

"Right."

"Come on, Jace is wearing a track in the carpet downstairs," Lilah laughs as she takes my hand and leads me downstairs to where Jace is pacing.

I snort as I take in the white suit he's wearing. It floats out as he turns and I take in the well defined bare chest that shows through the gaping fabric. *Better than Kevin from Grimsby* I think, remembering the popular professional from the BBC show. Jace stops dead still when he sees us at the bottom of the stairs, his gaze roaming over my whole body. "Ally, just wow." His voice is rough, making me blush at the heat I see in his eyes.

Glancing down, I look away from what I see in them. He's my best friend, no matter how much he feels about me, I will not cross that line. Lysais' eyes flash in my mind, reminding me I had enough boy problems and didn't need any more.

"You two ready?" Lilah's voice thankfully breaks the tension and lets me raise my head.

"Yeah," I nod and walk towards Jace.

The clearing is massive as we break through the trees. A bonfire is set up in the centre, ringed by small multi-coloured jars, each one containing a candle. As my gaze travels up, I find more of the jars suspended in the air. My jaw drops open as I marvel at the magical display. Jace gently tugs on my hand, drawing my attention to the clearing and all the people in it.

It seems that everyone from the village is here. Everyone is dressed in white, the men dressed like Jace and the women in different white dresses. None, I notice, are as intricate as the one I'm wearing, but the young women all have make up like mine, which makes me relax a little more as music starts up from somewhere in the trees.

Children giggle as they run past, chasing each other and generally getting under foot, as we make our way closer to where Agnes and Aradia stand together. Nerves begin building with each step I take closer, and I feel my erratic magic respond to my heightened emotions. Closing my eyes I will it to remain silent and still, trying to keep control.

"Ah the guest of honour," Aradia's motherly voice soothes my magic and my mind. Opening my eyes I look into her green ones and smile as her hand closes over mine, "how are you feeling?"

"Nervous," I answered honestly, making her smile.

"That is to be expected child." Agnes' sharp voice interrupts whatever her daughter was about to say, "and where is that child of yours Aradia?" She reprimands Charleene's absence.

"I'm here, Grandma," Charleene answers, as she drags a reluctant Dina towards our small group.

"Oh great, she brought the vampire," Agnes sneers, before

leaving us to talk to another group of witches.

"Will she ever get over it?" Charleene grumbles, staring daggers at her Grandmother's back.

"She will, in time, accept your decision Charleene," Aradia answers, "She just needs time, you're forcing us to turn our back on a thousand years of tradition with your...relationship." Smiling, she turns to Dina, "welcome and blessed be Dina," she says pleasantly before leaving us as well.

"Well she needs to hurry up." Charleene mutters quietly.

"Maybe I should go?" Dina asks.

"Don't you dare, it's a party, why shouldn't we get to enjoy it together?" Charleene's question is rhetorical, so none of us answer.

"Sooooo?" I ask, breaking the uncomfortable silence left behind, "who wants a drink?"

"Me, definitely me," Charleene answers, shaking her head before turning and striding to a long table set up with different bottles.

The music gets louder as the evening draws on and, once the sky is dark, I feel as if I'm back in Society, as the music pulses through my body. All around me, witches dance and drink together, enjoying the celebrations. I laugh as I catch a glimpse of Jace, caught in the middle of three young witches as they dance around him.

The ritual to break my father's spell is at midnight, but that's hours away still. Sighing, I tip another concoction of Charleene's down my throat. I don't know what she puts in them, but they taste amazing. My head spins as the alcohol in it begins to take effect, and I feel my hips begin to sway to the music as I close my eyes.

"Want to dance Princess?" Ly's voice whispers, making me smile as I remember him.

"If only you were here," I whisper to the night, before my eyes snap open when I feel hands on my waist.

"What if I was?" I feel his breath fan over the side of my face, making me shiver as his arm snakes around me, and his body steps up flush with mine. For a moment I lock eyes with Jace, as he battles through the crowd to get to me. "You look beautiful." Ly's voice snaps my attention back to him as his hand burns through the thin silk of my dress.

One hand presses against my stomach, as the other closes around my throat, forcing my head up. Looking at the stars, his cool breath tickles the nape of my neck, making me shiver in the already cold air. "Last time we were this close together you tried to kill me!" I snap up at the twinkling stars.

His growl reverberates through my back, I should be scared of the wildness in it but I'm not. "That wasn't..." Ly makes a choking sound behind my ear, as his smooth drawl cuts off. "I'm glad you didn't die Princess." He whispers, running his nose up and down my neck, causing goosebumps to erupt all over my skin.

His fingers tighten around my throat, but my heart told me he wouldn't hurt me, even after the fact that he'd been instrumental in my stabbing. Apparently you're just dumb! My head laughs at me, until his fingers dig in a little more and she purrs at both his force of dominance and the hard ridge currently rubbing against my arse through the thin dress. His rather impressive length presses harder into me as my underwear becomes a fricking swimming pool. More desire builds inside me from each point our bodies touch. My body seems to know Lysais even if my mind doesn't as it responds to him making my back arch.

"Lysais," I whisper, hearing the desire humming beneath my words, as my eyes stay fixed to the sky, even when his thumb strokes the soft column of my throat, "why are you here?" I force out around a moan.

"For you," he states, his breath tickling my ear, as his hands disappear from my body briefly, before closing around my shoulders, spinning me around on the spot. My hair whips across my face, leaving a brief sting, and then I'm staring up into his eyes as his shadows wrap around us both.

"No Alyssa!" I hear Jace's panicked scream, seconds before Ly's shadows block the world out, and I feel like I'm falling. Lysais' eyes and his hands are the only thing keeping me upright.

My stomach rolls as I feel solid ground beneath my feet. Confused, I glance around the cave we're now standing in. Water drips into a small pool and stalactites drop from the ceiling, illuminated by the small sphere of blueish, white light that Lysais hangs in the air above us.

Shadows twist and turn around him as he stares down at me, his eyes shadowed but no longer cold and distant. Desire floods my body as I see the fire in his eyes. They run down my barely there white dress, chosen to honour the witch's celebration, drinking me in and leaving a trail of fire in their wake.

Forcing my eyes away from his face, I run them up and down the tight black leather covering his toned arms, chest and legs. Leaving nothing to the imagination as it moulds to his skin. My gaze roams over the assortment of weapons strapped to his powerful body. Shivering, I finally reached out, running my finger gently across his full bottom lip.

"I've missed you Alysium." He whispers against my finger, confusing me before his warm lips touch mine, setting free the inferno raging inside me. Forgetting everything but the feel of his lips dancing with mine, he deepens the kiss, making me gasp. As soon as my lips part, his tongue sweeps inside, tangling forcefully with mine as our pent-up passion takes control.

My hand slides across his cheek, round the back of his neck and moves up, until I've got a fistful of his dark hair, pulling his head back slightly to make him growl. His fangs brush my tongue as it darts in and out of his mouth, and tingles race along my nerves. Gasping, a moan escapes my mouth as his moves to my neck, kissing a trail down to my collar bones, lavishing them with attention before he moves his lips lower, until he reaches the edge of my corset, forcing him to pause with a devilish smile as he glances up at me.

Ly sucks one of my nipples into his warm wet mouth through the thin material, making my eyes close as I gasp. He grips the side of my bodice in his strong hands, before tearing the fabric in two, leaving my chest bare. I moan louder and grip his head tighter, as his mouth returns to my bare skin. His tongue moves in tantalising patterns, soft then hard, as I make noises I've never made before.

Suddenly, cold air flashes across my nipple, making it harden as he moves to the other, giving it the same devoted attention and forcing another moan past my lips as I feel myself get wetter. "Is it really you Ly?" I gasp needing confirmation that my Ly is here with me, not the cold stranger I've seen him become.

His growl reverberates through my chest as he scents my arousal, and heat plunges from my stomach to my vagina. Smiling against my skin, "it's me Princess," he reassures me, "I would never let anyone touch you like this. They'd die first!" He snarls against my skin as his hands gently caress down my back, making me arch against his hungry mouth, until he's gripping my arse through the dress that now hangs around my waist.

Pulling his mouth away from my skin, I groan in disappointment, and tug on his head, needing to feel his lips on me as the fire rages inside, but I'm no match for his strength as he pushes me back. Frowning I move towards him wanting—*no needing*—to feel his warmth against me.

"Patience," he murmurs with a sinful smile, stopping me in my tracks as I watch him begin to remove all his weapons. The thud as they hit the floor, one at a time, makes me squirm with impatience. Pushing the dress over my hips, I watch his eyes darken as I step out of it and run my hands down my body.

I've never been so bold in all of my life—*that I can remember* —as I run my hands across my nipples, pinching them before moving down across my stomach, until I slip my hand between my legs. I moan as I stare into his blue eyes and my finger slides against the wetness he's helped create.

With two steps Ly closes the gap between us, his hands grip my arse tightly as he lifts me from the floor. Wrapping my legs around his waist is torture as I feel all of his muscles move against the inside of my legs and my pussy grinds against his hard cock still trapped in his trousers.

I whimper as he moves us both to the floor of the cave. He's beneath me, watching as I straddle his waist, my knees digging into the hard floor. A coy smile plays on my lips, as I look down at this powerful man submitting to me.

"I'm all yours Ally." He whispers, making my desire fan higher.

Running my hands up his muscled chest, I find the zip to his leather jacket, and slowly pull it down, exposing him to me as I wiggle against his cock. My smile widens as he lets a groan slip from between his lips, as I run my nails over his skin and his cock twitches where it's still trapped in his trousers. His hands tighten around my waist, and it's the only warning I get before I'm laid on my back staring up at him.

"My turn." He explains, his voice deep and sexy before he moves down my body, placing kisses on my skin as he goes.

God, this man and his mouth, I think before his tongue reaches out and licks up my soaking pussy. His tongue traces my folds gently, my mind going blank as I focus on what he's doing to me. *No man could ever make me feel like this* I realise, as I hear my moans echo around us. Moaning and wriggling against his mouth, I let go as tingles race across every inch of my skin. I scream to the roof as he sucks my clit into his mouth, and the most intense orgasm—that I can imagine—crashes over me.

Ly continues licking and sucking as I come down, making me twitch against his mouth as it teases my over sensitive flesh. He moves away as my moans turn to whimpers, and when my eyes finally open I'm staring into his blue ones.

"That...that...I have no words." I stammer out, my brain not working. He smiles at my lack of words before slipping his jacket off.

"That was just the start Princess," He growls before crushing his mouth to mine. I moan when I taste myself on his lips, and frantically move my hands to his trousers wanting them gone.

Breaking the kiss, he glances down at me, smiling and my control snaps. "Off Now!" I demand when I can't find the button.

"As you wish." He states around a laugh, before undoing and pushing his trousers down. All thoughts flee my mind, as I take in his cock as it springs free. He's huge. My mouth goes dry, as I glance from it to his face and back again, before swallowing.

Reaching out slowly, I run my hand up his beautiful cock, making him hiss as my fingers gently explore the soft hardness. Growing bolder with each noise he makes, I wrap my hand around him and tug hard. Smiling when he groans—it sounds tortured—and makes me look at his face. My smile grows as I take in his heated eyes. Pushing myself up, I keep my eyes locked on his as I lick from his balls to his tip.

Ly's hips jerk forward as his hand fists into my hair. Opening wide, I let him push inside my mouth and moan as he fills me. He pulls out slowly, before pushing back a bit deeper. As he pulls back my tongue traces the underside of him, making him shiver and groan.

"Ally I'm going to..." he doesn't get time to finish before he's cumming, the saltiness coating my tongue as I swallow it down.

Smiling, I lean back and open my legs, showing him how wet I am and what I want. With a growl he moves impossibly fast, until he's braced above me, my wrists trapped in one of his hands as his other steadies his fully hard cock. I guess Fae don't need a recovery time I think, as he's pushing slowly inside me. My moan rips from my throat as I feel every inch of him. He settles inside me, pausing for a second to let me adjust to his size, before he slides out of me and slams back in.

Ly sets a punishing pace as he fucks me, but I couldn't care less, as my back scraps against the stone, the small bite of pain heightening the pleasure I feel with each thrust. I can feel the orgasm building inside me as my pussy clamps down around his cock, milking it with every thrust as he hits that sweet spot over and over and over, as I scream my pleasure.

"Alysium!" He bellows as he cums. Pushing me over the edge, I scream his name before I fall into an abyss of pure pleasure as I see stars and my chest pulses in time with his—it's like we're connected heart to heart.

Soft kisses rouse me, as Ly mumbles sweet nothing's against my cheek, making me smile as I blink my eyes open.

"Hey beautiful," he murmurs before kissing me gently.

"Mmmm, hello to you too," I whisper as he pulls back, "What time is it?" I ask, fearing that our time together is coming to an end.

Ly smiles sadly before answering, confirming my suspicion, "2am."

"Don't go?" I gasp out knowing he's about to say goodbye again, but I don't know why. My attention is on Ly as he turns calmly toward me, his eyes shining with sadness as he looks down into my eyes.

"Forgive me." He whispers, his eyes tortured before I feel his magic invade my mind and I'm lost. The cave disappears as I watch memories play out under my closed eyelids.

Me as a young girl, twirling around in circles as my newest dress flares out around my legs. Me laughing with Jace, as we're both forced to learn sword fighting, martial arts, politics of court. You name it we learned it. My dreams slot into the stream of memories, blending in seamlessly so that they now make sense.

The faint tugging in my chest that has always connected me to Ly snaps strongly into place, as I remember who he is to me. My Prince of Shadows, my protector, friend, enemy...my eyes fly open as I realise what my body has been trying to tell me.

Lysais is my soul bonded mate!

Chapter Twenty-Six

Alyssa.

My eyes blink open and I find myself laying on a soft bed, instead of the cave. Glancing around the vaguely familiar room I'm in, I try to come to terms with everything I've learnt about myself. I don't know what Ly did, but my father's block has weakened considerably. I remember. *I'm not human but I'm also not a monster.*

I'm a freaking fairy princess! I groan to myself silently. What the hell?

Jumping from the bed and running to the full length mirror, I gaze at my reflection.

Meeting my violet gaze in the mirror I stare in wonder at the face that looks back. My hair looks like it's on fire as the red strands drift on an invisible wind, my delicately pointed ears poke through startling me and my eyes...*Oh my god!* I think as I stare into my now violet eyes.

Strength courses through my muscles as I let my eyes run down the rest of the body shown in the mirror. My new—*or is it my old*—lithe body is wrapped in supple leather, that moves effortlessly with my body. *I look like a badass,* I think smiling at my reflection as something begins to tickle inside my mind.

Focusing within I feel my chaotic elemental magic settle down, and for the first time since it reawakened weeks ago I feel in control. Smiling, I call upon my fire and watch as a ball begins spinning above my open hand. Opening the other, I laugh as I make a ball of water. Wanting both magics away, I watch as they harmlessly fade.

I'm in control. I marvel as I feel the playful energy of it inside me. Letting it out, I watch in wonder as multi-coloured ribbons dance around my body.

"Well look who's back," Jace's voice interrupts my play, but the ribbons continue dancing. "Beautiful," he mutters, as he watches my magic before dropping to the floor and bowing his head and declaring, "welcome back Princess."

"Get up Jace." I whisper, meeting his eyes as he lifts his head and smiles, before turning to a package propped up next to the door.

"Lilah left you these." He says the words, picking the package up and handing it to me. It's heavy, I realise, as I hold it and walk to the bed. "What is it?" I ask him as I lay it down.

"Just open it."

Carefully, I unwrap the cloth and gasp, as I reveal each weapon that's been carefully wrapped. Glancing up at Jace briefly, before staring back down at the long thin sword and daggers. "They're mine," I state as I run my hand down the suddenly familiar blade, "I remember." I mumble more to myself than to him.

"Everything?" His question shocks me into looking up at him as he searches my gaze, "Lysais?"

"I don't know what he did, but he unlocked my mind," I state, watching Jace take in what I've just said.

"And how do you feel," he pauses, searching my eyes again, "about him, I mean?"

I think over his question carefully, as I examine my feelings for Ly. I remember how his touch and voice makes me shiver, how his eyes hold me captive when he looks at me. I feel myself blush as I remember all the times he touched me in the past. I love him. I realise as I look at Jace, "I...I..." I try to speak, not able to find the words to answer his question.

Jace looks away from me before I can fully see the emotion my reaction causes. "Ally, we need to go," he states, staring at the door. "Put your weapons on, you're going to need them." His voice is distant as he refuses to look at me.

"Jace..." I begin, reaching out to him with my hand, but he moves away before I can touch him. "What's wrong?" I ask, needing to know what I've done wrong.

"Nothing. Come on," he says, still not looking at me as he walks to the door.

Quickly strapping the leather sheath to my back, I carefully slide the sword into it, feeling its familiar weight settle against my spine. Then, I place each dagger into the hidden sheaths along my arms and legs. Once every weapon is in place, I feel lethal as I turn and follow Jace from the room. I stare at his back as he leads us through the house and outside into the sunshine.

I notice how quiet the small village is, gone are the noises of life from before, "Jace? What's going on?" I ask, taking in the vacant houses around us, "where is everyone?"

Confused, I make myself walk faster until I'm level with him, as faint noises stir the air. Jace looks at me calmly before answering, "they're fighting."

"Fighting who?" I ask, dreading the answer, but needing to know.

"Demorans." He responds coldly, as fear snakes its way up my back, and my eyes widen as the noises become louder. I can hear the sound of screams, and metal hitting metal in the distance as we leave the village behind. My steps quicken as I run up the hill, needing to see what my ears are telling me. At the top I freeze, staring across the raging battle .

The witches fight in groups, fending off the hoard of Demoran around them. My gaze darts quickly from each small group, as they try and fail to protect themselves.

"Ready to go hunting?" Jace asks, pulling a deadly looking sword free from his hip, breaking into my horror. I nod once before calling my magic to me, and setting my sights on a group of terrified witches. Then we're running down the hill towards the fighting.

The sounds are deafening, as I throw fire and water at another shadow demon that blinks into existence before me. It feels like I've been fighting for hours as more and more shadow demons come for me. Spinning around, I look once again for any of my friends as my sword connects with another Demoran's heart, making it scream before vanishing.

All the training I was given before being sent here, kicked in the moment I was submersed in the demons, transforming my every movement into a lethal dance as I fight for my life.

Glancing around me again, I try to find Jace. He'd been beside me moments ago, fighting to keep us both alive until five Demoran forced us apart. "Argggg!" I scream, as white-hot pain blinds me for a second, as a shadow blade shoves through my right shoulder, forcing me to focus on my own fight instead of searching. Anger rises alongside my magic, my emotions fueling it, combining elements in a protective ring around me, pushing the shadows back.

I hate this, I realise, catching my breath in the circle of quiet I've created. A memory tries to surface, of another attack just like this one, but I push it to the back of my mind as my hand tightens on my sword.

Smiling, I recall my many lessons on fighting with weapons, magic and how Lysais taught me to run my elemental magic down my weapons to make them more powerful against his kind. I'm running magic down my blade as my bubble of space pops, and without thinking I'm moving.

My sword slashes through the air, meeting the shadow blade that was aiming for my arm, with a snarl I push him back and duck the next blade aimed for my head. Rolling forwards and springing back up to my feet, I spin, dragging my blade through the shadow's stomach and hearing its unearthly roar as my fire coated blade cuts him in half.

Searching for my next target, I'm not disappointed when I see Jace surrounded by shadows and begin moving towards him. As I draw closer, a shadow blade cuts through Jace's leather armor as he defends against four other shadow demons. I let out a snarl as I noticed other cuts marring him, and the silver blood coating him.

Then I'm running, stabbing, slicing at anything that comes at me. I cast my magic on instinct, as I make my way closer and closer to Jace, taking out any Demoran that's between us. Snarling, I spin lining my back against his as we look out over the clearing I've made. My anger rises further as I watch the witches of the coven fighting for their own lives. Their magic creating rainbows in the air as the sound of swords meeting deafens me again. The battle rages on, never ending as snarls and screams echo around me as I take it all in.

"There's no end to them." I snarl at Jace, as I take another demon's head from his shoulders.

"We need to do something." He responds by darting around me to stab a demon I hadn't seen.

We need something big I think, as I let my hate and anger boil through my veins, at the senseless violence around me. How can the Shadow King condone this? I wonder even as I'm grabbing every strand of elemental magic I possess, forcing it to build as I instinctively block the physical attacks from touching me, or Jace at my back.

I can feel my power burning through me as I struggle to keep it contained, until I've built up enough. My mind splits, one side focusing on building power, and the other on fighting to keep me alive as I lay imaginary targets on each shadow demon here. I'm barely aware that I'm glowing as everyone turns towards me, the battle pausing before I scream.

Bands of magic burst from me as I meet the now terrified gazes of shadow demons. Fire, water, air and earth shoot out from me in glowing strands, as I smile vindictively. The earth opens up, swallowing demons as my fire burns them to ash. I watch as my water turns the field to mud, as it covers demons, trapping them until the witches can finish them off. My hair swirls around me as the air protects me and Jace from any demon that tries to hurt us.

My body burns at the overuse of magic, as it takes my energy to fuel the power rushing out of me. Suddenly I feel a pop inside my mind and sense foreign magic rage inside me.

It's not like my elemental magic, this magic's different, it feels alive as it batters against my mind. Darkness closes over me for a second before I push it away, watching the last shadow demon fall, as a pressure builds painfully behind my eyes.

It's all I can think about as it bashes against invisible walls inside my head. Grabbing my head, I scream in agony as the magic tries to rip apart my mind. My knees smash into the grass, as arms wrap around me, pulling me against a hard chest. Jace's familiar scent of cherries and fresh air surrounds me as I open my eyes, locking them on to Jace's familiar brown ones, trying to anchor myself to something, anything, as my mind splits apart.

"What's happening to me Jace?" I ask him terrified, as the pain settles before rising again.

"I don't know Ally." He murmurs not taking his eyes from mine as they fill with tears.

"It hurts," I whimper as he holds me. "Please, please make it stop!" I scream as the pressure gets worse again, forcing my eyes shut as I concentrate on breathing slowly, as though that will help.

I feel myself connect to everything around me as my magic flares, trying to find whatever is attacking me. I feel the witches surrounding us but can't open my eyes as another wave of pain makes me scream.

"What do you want?" Jace's snarl has my eyes flying open, but I can't turn my head to see who he's glaring at.

From the tug in my chest, I know who's here before he speaks, "I'm here to help Jacin," his deep growl makes me shiver. Even through the pain inside my head, I feel desire stirring in response to him. *I don't fully understand why my body reacts so much to him, or why Jace seems to hate him but I'm glad he's here.*

Trying to smile, I force my head to follow his voice, somehow knowing that if I can just see his eyes the pain won't be so bad. My head rocks on Jace's arm but I still can't see him. Another increase in the pressure has me screaming out, everything but the pain fading into the distance as I try to breath through it.

I barely feel the cool tears falling over my cheeks, or the new set of strong arms that now hold me. The scent of smoke, leather and lavender surrounds me making my body relax and when I next open my eyes, I see his ice blue ones and smile weakly.

"Hey," I whisper as he gently moves the strands of hair stuck to my forehead.

"Let go Princess," He whispers back, in his commanding tone.

"Let go of what?" I question him, wondering what I'm meant

to let go of.

"Alysium, let down your walls," staring up into his eyes I see desperation shining in them. "Concentrate."

Nodding, I try ignoring the pain coursing through my skull but can't. "I can't Ly," I whimper, "the pain's too bad." Fresh tears fall over my cheeks faster than he can wipe them away.

"You can do this Ally," he whispers, bending toward me. Searching his eyes for his intentions, I gasp as his lips meet mine. Stunned for a moment, I freeze, before relaxing further into his hold and kissing him back. His lips are warm and gentle as they move with mine, his tongue darting inside the instant I open my mouth with a gasp. Tingles flood my body as his tongue dances with mine. Ly swallows the small gasps and moans I make, as he distracts me from everything but him.

Mine! My voice whispers possessively through my mind as I forget the pain and focus on his lips.

Then I'm no longer in Ly's arms but laying on a hard floor, bright rainbows dancing around me as a bright archway shimmers next to me. Staring at it in wonder, I watch as flickers roll over it and I see a city with tall buildings reaching into the sky, then it shifts again to a barren landscape covered in shadows with a red sky and mountains in the distance.

"Alysium!" Mother's voice drags my attention away from the arch as she runs toward me. "No, no, no." She repeats as she reaches me and collapses next to my head.

"What's happening to me?" I ask confused.

"It's going to be ok," She mutters, touching my cheek gently, her gaze glancing at the arch and back to me. "Alysium you need to listen to me." Nodding, I focus on her and only her, "you need to contain it."

"How?" I ask, trusting her judgment.

"Wrap it inside your elemental magic."

Closing my eyes I turn my attention inward, focusing on the colourful strands of my elements. Ribbons of red, blue, green, gold and silver twirl and dance inside my mind, and I feel their gentle, playful energy caress my body.

"Good, that's good Alysium, now search for a bright white spark and build the strongest walls you can around it." Following her advice I search the part of my mind that my magic comes from. Shifting through the ribbons until suddenly it's there. A ball of pure white light, like that surrounding the archway shimmers. Focusing upon it, I grab the red ribbon and begin to wrap it around the ball, then repeat the same process until the ball of light can barely be seen through the shifting rainbow of elements.

Opening my eyes I watch as the archway I created dims, until it finally disappears. Once it's gone I look at her, willing her with my eyes to explain what just happened.

"Alysium, no one can know you have this power," Her stern voice echoes around the empty chamber.

"Why?" I question wondering what's so bad about it, "what is it?"

"You can make gates to the other worlds" She explains, "but it's dangerous,"

Startled gasps drag me from the memory and back to the here and now, as I feel the walls I'd built around the magic crumble. Then it's flooding from me, taking the pressure and pain with it, as my eyes flash open, meeting Lysais' inches from mine. Searching his blue eyes I watch as shadows grow inside them, and he inches away from me.

"Find me." He whispers before pushing me away, back into Jace's arms. But I don't care about that, all I care about is that he's leaving me. Confused, I grab onto his shirt, trying to hold him to me as his eyes turn cold and distant, dimming to a dull grey as he pries my fingers from his shirt.

"Ly?" I gasp as he turns from me and begins walking away, leaving me, "Stop!" My voice rings out loud and clear, command ringing in it that makes his steps pause.

He looks back at me once before his gaze travels to something behind me, following his eyes I gasp at the archway shimmering behind Jace's head. "Goodbye Princess." He manages to snap at me, forcing me to look back at him. His eye suddenly cold and hard, as I hear my Father's voice ringing through my mind:

"Red, blue, bronze and green,
magic threads remain unseen,
hide our daughter from his sight,
until her power burns too bright!

Yellow, brown, silver, pink,
give my daughter time to think,
as He searches high and low,
steady times rushing flow.

Orange, peach and indigo,
to disguise her inner-glow,
steal the memories from her mind,
to leave a trace would be unkind.

Black, gold, grey and white,
keep her safe from His delight,
protect her heart until she knows,
the truth, the perils and her foes."

Shaking my head, I stare at Lysais watching as his demeanor changes, and he begins clapping. "So it's true," he snarls at me as I cower back. I don't like this side of Ly, he's different. Cold, indifferent—not my Ly my brain tells me—as a scream pierces the silence that's descended.

Lilah's war-cry has my eyes darting from Ly. She's running, shoving people aside with her sword at her waist, aimed right at Ly, "Murderer, get away from her," she screams.

I stare, unable to move as she nears Ly and his smile turns evil, "Lilah, no!" I scream, able to do nothing else as I watch Ly's blade draws backwards as he laughs. "Again? They do love to protect you Princess," He sneers at me, as a new memory plays out inside my head.

I'm alone, standing in a ring of Demoran, that keep everyone back. My gaze skips from Jace's furious eyes, to mother's worried ones when gasps and murmurs break through the silence. My eyes are drawn across from me as the ring of shadow demons opens to let someone through. No, not just someone, Ly.

He strides toward me, each step oozing confidence as my lips begin to smile. He'll save me, I think for a moment, before I take in his cold, flat stare. Glancing down at his familiar body I notice the weapons strapped to him and take a step back.

"Lysais?" I question, frowning at him as he draws nearer. From the corner of my eyes I see Mother and Father straining against the Fae that hold them, before my eyes return to Lysais.

"You're coming with me Princess." He states coldly, closing the distance and sliding one of his shadow blades free from its sheath with a metallic swish.

"Why?" I cry, confused as he raises the blade toward me and I realise he's with them. "You vowed to protect me!" I scream at him, but he doesn't get the chance to answer as Arielle breaks free and runs between us screaming.

Everything slows down as her scream cuts off with a gurgle, my hands close on the tops of her arms, her mouth now opening and closing silently. Slowly I turn her sideways as my eyes drop down to her stomach. No, No, No! My mind is screaming as I see Ly's shadow blade sinking through her thin body.

Then the screaming starts as I watch Arielle's blue blood seep into her white dress, staining the silk around the blade. Following the arm back to Lysais, my heart shatters as I realise this is real.

He's betrayed me!

Tears course over my cheeks as I stare at the Lysais walking away from me as a sob breaks from my mouth. Making him stop and turn back to me. Searching his cold eyes I'm trying to reconcile the two versions of him that I now clearly remember. The kind protector and the traitor. Which is the real him? I try to figure it out as my eyes dart between his. I feel my heart split in two again as the last of my father's magic leaves my mind and I see it on repeat, his sword aiming for me. I'd given him my heart, thinking I could trust him with it.

How could he betray me? I wonder, staring into his cold blue eyes trying to find the answer.

"Why?" I choke out between my sobs, but he doesn't answer. I don't feel Jace standing with me, focusing solely on Ly, "Why!" I scream again at him as Jace walks backwards, pulling me into the gate. Darkness closes around me for a second before I stumble out into a different world.

Looking up, I recognise the stars above me and shiver as the feeling of belonging sings through my blood. My tears keep falling even as a warm breeze blows my now flame red hair in front of my eyes and I know I'm home.

The end for now...

* * *

Thank You

Thank you for reading the first book in The Gatemaker Series, I hope that you enjoyed meeting Alyssa, Jacin and Lysais as much as I loved writing about the start of their journeys. If you'reexcited to keep following them, then their adventures will continue in Book 2 Of Fairies & Fiends coming Autumn 2023.

However please don't be dismayed as Dina and Charleene's story will continue in the first book of their own Dark Desires Series coming Summer 2023. Where we will get to know these two fiesty females more. We'll follow them through their own troubles and strife as they try to peice together Charleene's past, while keeping her out of the evil hands hunting her. Will she be responsible for dooming the world or saving it?

Acknowledgement

I would like to say thank you to all of my readers, being an author would not be possible without those willing to pick up and read our books.

To my dear friend and editor Ashlie thank you so much for reading each draft, reassuring my every doubt, (especially when that pesky inner voice told me to quit,) for all the endless questions and for overall helping me get this book written. You are one in a million and i could not have told this story without you.

I would also like to thank my Beta reader Maggie Hand, you have helped tweak this novel into the book it is today. I can not thank you enough.

To my ARC Readers you are imperative to authors and our books, thank you for taking the time to read Of Magic & Lies.

Thank you to Getcover_Design for my beautiful cover art.

Lastly I would like to thank everyone in my life that has believed, encouraged and supported me to realise my dream of becoming a published author. Thank you for listening to me rabbit on about characters and plots that only I could see in my head.

Afterword

Please, please, please if you enjoyed this book then take the five minutes to leave me a review on Amazon, Goodreads or even on my social media pages. Reviews are so important to author as they help other readers find and wish to read our books. Leaving one will help authors to keep creating the books you love so much.

You can also follow me on social media.

Facebook- Author Maggie Brown

Also you can join my facebook reader group Maggie's Minions

Instagram- @authorm.brown

Tiktok- @authormaggiebrown

About The Author

Maggie Brown

 Maggie Brown is an author from the North East of England, where she lives with her family. Maggie enjoys writing stories that center around magical and mystical beings, such as Fae, Witches, Vampires and more.

Books By This Author

Memories At Midnight

When the past comes back to haunt you.

Welcome to Wintergreen Manor.

After mum's tragic accident, I didn't think my life could possibly get any worse. But it does when dad announces we're moving! Away from my friends, school, the house I grew up in but worse of all my memories of mum.

Leaving London far behind to go and live on the East Coast in the tiny town of Filey, should be a dream. However from the first mention of Wintergreen Manor I only see it as a living nightmare.

It's isolated, stuck in the past, and Oh yeah, the place is haunted...yeah you heard correctly haunted! As in real ghosts, things that go bump in the night, blooming heck even my dreams are haunted by the ghosts of long dead people.

This place is full of secrets and a hidden history that wants to come to light, but why does it have to be me? Urggg, I hate it here, but there is one saving grace to Wintergreen Manor and that's Lucas. He's hot as hell, with his brown hair, hazel eyes and sun kissed skin. But he totally hates me, even though we've never met before.

Can he move past his hate and help me uncover the truth buried in my family's past? Or is history doomed to repeat itself, with me as the victim?

I am Rosemary Wintergreen and this is our story!

Printed in Great Britain
by Amazon